The world is in peril.

An ancient evil is rising from beneath
Erdas, and we need YOU to help stop it.

Claim your spirit animal and _____ the
adventure.

1. Go to schola_____

2. Log _____
   _____

3. Hav_____ enter the
   code _____ck the adventure.

You_ Code: NNC4MRFDXH

By the Four Fallen,
The Greencloaks

scholastic.com/spiritanimals

I know this is difficult,
but I need you to trust me.
To trust us.

THE RETURN

Varian Johnson

SCHOLASTIC INC.

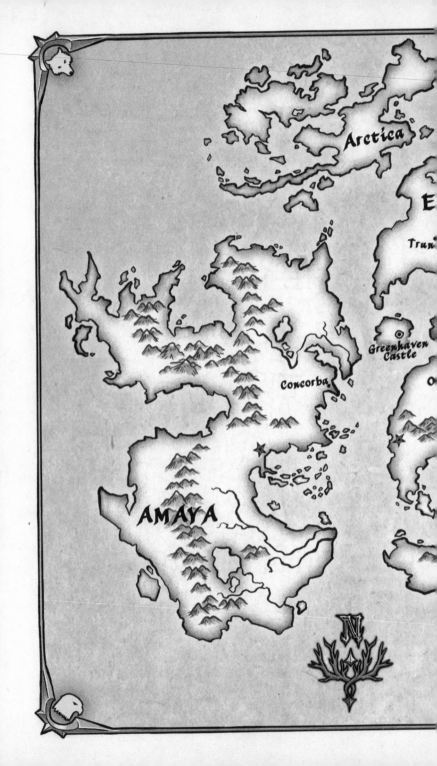

Arctica

E

Tran'

Greenhaven
Castle

O

Concorba

AMAYA

N

ERDAS

The Petral Mountains

ZHONG

Jano Rion

OCEANUS

LO

The Evertree

Hundred Isles

Stetriol

For Savannah, Sydney, Elisabeth, Adrienne,
Daniel, Tex, John Marcus, Aidan, and Nadia.
And for Theo and Sebastian, two dogs that never
met an apple they didn't like.
—V. J.

Library of Congress Control Number: 2015956411

ISBN 978-0-545-84207-5

10 9 8 7 6 5 4 3 2 1   16 17 18 19 20

Book design by Charice Silverman
First edition, May 2016

Printed in the U.S.A. 23

Scholastic US: 557 Broadway • New York, NY 10012
Scholastic Canada: 604 King Street West • Toronto, ON M5V 1E1
Scholastic New Zealand Limited: Private Bag 94407 • Greenmount, Manukau 2141
Scholastic UK Ltd.: Euston House • 24 Eversholt Street • London NW1 1DB

1

ZERIF

ERIF JAMMED HIS FINGERS INTO A SMALL CREVICE AND climbed onto the narrow, rocky ledge. Ahead, the majestic peaks of the Kenjoba Mountains stretched before him. Below, he could still hear the shouts of the Niloan warriors and Greencloaks in pursuit. They had been chasing him for days. He thought that he would be able to hide in one of the villages in South Nilo, but it had only taken a few days for someone to turn on him and alert the authorities. He bolted as soon as he saw the first Greencloak roaming the small village.

Now that the war was over, Zerif found that very few of his allies remained. Most of the Conquerors had surrendered as soon as they lost control over their spirit animals, thanks to the destruction of the Evertree canceling the effects of Gerathon's Bile. The few warriors that still pledged allegiance to the Reptile King wanted nothing to do with Zerif–and would have probably turned him over to the Greencloaks themselves if they found him.

Not even Zerif's jackal remained. Like the other animals, it had abandoned him as soon as he lost his power to control it.

He was glad that he hadn't bothered to name it.

No matter, he thought. *I am Zerif. I will triumph again. As always.*

Zerif climbed to another ledge, scraping his hands and face as he pulled himself up. His blue tunic, ripped and withered, flapped against him in the howling winds. The breeze shifted direction, and suddenly the stench of rot filled Zerif's nostrils. He looked around. To his right, on another ledge, large black buzzards picked at the remains of an animal. Zerif backed up to gain as much running ground as possible. Then he took off, his weakened legs flailing as he leaped through the air. He landed on the ledge and stumbled, almost falling over into the deep, empty valley below. Once he was sure of his footing, he charged toward the birds, driving them away.

Zerif peered at the rotting carcass. There wasn't much left of the wild dog—a few slivers of flesh hung on the otherwise dry bones, and the beast's fur was torn and ripped. Still, he picked up what remained of the animal and flung it over his shoulder. One of the Greencloaks had been traveling with a fox; he hoped the dead animal would help mask his own scent.

After a few more hours of climbing, Zerif stumbled upon a long fissure in the rock face. It took some effort, but he crawled through. Sparse patches of green moss covered the slick, cool walls of the small cavern. The cave was barely big enough for him to sit up in, much less stand. He was shivering so much that his teeth rattled and his fingers were blue, but he didn't dare light a fire.

Anger seethed from him. This was not what was supposed to happen when he allied himself with the Conquerors. They had failed him.

Zerif dropped the carcass beside him and curled himself into a tight ball. He would wait and plan. Eventually, the Greencloaks would abandon their pursuit.

And then, very soon, he would be great and powerful once again.

Two days later, he still hadn't crawled out of the cave.

Every time he considered leaving, he thought he heard the footsteps of Greencloaks or the shouts of Niloan warriors. Perhaps it was just the wind. Or the sound of rocks tumbling down the mountain. Maybe he was hallucinating. He had tried to eat moss to gain strength but had retched the bitter vegetation back up as soon as it hit his stomach.

It was there, lying with his face pressed against the ground, that he first saw the gray worm inching toward him.

It was small and strange-looking. And fluid—almost like a coil of smoke. It moved toward him with an eerie purpose, as if it knew he was there. Zerif had never seen anything like it.

What is this? A leech? A snail?

And is it edible?

Zerif shook his head as he considered what do to. *Has the mighty Zerif fallen so low that the idea of eating a worm excites him?*

He picked up the worm, hoping to study it. It wriggled up his hand much quicker than he had anticipated. Before he knew it, it was at his elbow. He shook his arm furiously, but the worm remained. It burrowed its way into a deep gash on Zerif's shoulder. Panicked, he hurled himself into the wall, hoping to crush the thing. When that didn't work, he picked up a jagged rock and tried to cut the worm out of his skin.

Nothing seemed to stop the creature. It inched its way beneath his skin, up to his collarbone, then neck, then face. Zerif could feel it writhing. He screamed—both in fear and in pain. He felt it curling at his forehead.

Zerif twisted, clawing at his face, driving deep gouges into his skin.

And then, Zerif fell silent. His legs and arms ceased to move. They no longer belonged to him.

Slowly, he heard ancient whispers echoing in his mind. Soft at first, they intensified, feeding the anger and evil already residing in the depths of his soul.

Power surged inside him. He rose to his feet, no longer hungry or pained. He sensed the voice telling him to leave. To travel north. A being of great power would be there. An eagle.

Halawir.

Suddenly, Zerif found himself surrounded by hundreds of small gray worms. They crept from rocks, seeping out like liquid darkness. Parasites. Allies.

With their help, Zerif would be great once again.

He would be feared and worshipped.

He would rule the world.

2

RIPPLES

T AKODA SAT AT THE EDGE OF THE SULFUR SEA. YELLOW, gritty water lapped onto his boots, seeping the worn leather, but he did not want to move inland. This location gave him the best view of the endless sea, the jagged cliffs, and the small strip of beach in between.

Takoda kept searching, hoping to catch a flash of Xanthe's pale skin or white hair. He knew she would find them. She had to. He refused to believe otherwise.

How long had it been since he'd last seen her, when they were running through the Arachane Fields? Hours? Days? Longer? Although he'd only known her for a short amount of time, Takoda had come to enjoy their long talks. She seemed just as fascinated about his life with the monks as he had been about hers belowground. She wasn't just their guide. She was their friend. *His* friend. And now she was gone. Just like his parents during the war.

Farther along the shoreline, Meilin and Conor hollowed out a large purple gourd. They'd found a field of them while exploring one of the cliff caves. The fruit reeked, almost making Takoda lose the little bit of food remaining in his stomach. But after an initial test, it looked like the hard shell could hold them all for a journey across the sea.

Takoda heard steps behind him but didn't turn around. Even the soft sand of the Sulfur Sea could not mute the heavy, lumbering footsteps of Kovo, the Great Beast. His spirit animal.

A few weeks ago, Takoda wouldn't have needed to rely on footsteps or snorts to know that Kovo was approaching. Before, Kovo's presence hovered just at the edge of his own thoughts. While strange in the beginning, Takoda had come to like the feeling. It reminded him of the quiet, constant buzz of a hummingbird as it neared a flower. But now, as the bonds between spirit animals and their human partners continued to stretch, he could hardly sense the ape anymore.

At first, Takoda thought this would be a blessing. If the bonds broke, perhaps he might finally be rid of Kovo, the cunning, treacherous mastermind responsible for Erdas's two great wars. But now, Takoda couldn't imagine life without him.

In addition, ever since bonding with Kovo, the anger and ache Takoda felt due to the deaths of his parents had dulled. It was there, but subdued. It didn't consume him. He could cope with it. But now, Xanthe's loss had amplified everything.

Kovo dropped a large handful of rockweed beside Takoda. Without Xanthe, Takoda and the others didn't know the difference between vegetation that would sustain them or would make them sick—or worse. Finally, Meilin had discovered a growth of rockweed during one of her explorations. Xanthe had shown them the strange weeds earlier in their journey and taught them how to eat it to draw out its nutrients. Xanthe was still saving them, even now that she was missing.

Kovo pushed Takoda's shoulder, causing the boy to look up and meet his gaze. Takoda was often surprised how gentle the Great Ape's touch could be. Once Kovo was sure he had Takoda's attention, he pinched his fingers and motioned to his mouth.

"Thank you," Takoda said. "But what about Conor and Meilin? Have they eaten?"

Takoda wasn't sure, but it almost looked like Kovo rolled his large red eyes at the mention of their companions.

Kovo and Meilin didn't like each other. They would never admit it, but they were similar in many ways. Both were leaders who *demanded* information, when asking would have been much simpler.

As far as Conor was concerned, Takoda wondered if Kovo had already given up on him. Conor's sickness worsened as each day passed. The parasite's journey up the boy's arm had slowed, but not stopped. It would soon overtake him.

Takoda picked up some of the rockweed and tried to give it back to the ape. "Kovo, they need to eat, too. And it would probably help them feel more comfortable around you if you were the one that offered it."

Kovo snorted, then returned back up the beach, knuckling toward the cliffs, his fists pounding into the beach. He kicked up sand as he walked away, covering the abandoned rockweed with grit and grime.

Takoda sighed as he rose to his feet. He shook as much sand from the rockweed as he could, then walked toward Conor and Meilin. He'd tried to help with cleaning the gourd earlier, but Meilin had sent him away when it became clear that Takoda was spending more time watching the sea than scraping away the stinking fruit.

Briggan leaped to his feet and playfully circled Takoda as he approached.

"Sorry, but no meat, I'm afraid," Takoda said.

Briggan whimpered, then returned to Conor's side. The wolf had remained close to Conor ever since the fire, even though Briggan appeared to dislike the feel of the black sand on his paws.

"Kovo found some more rockweed," Takoda said to Conor. Sweat covered Conor's forehead, and Takoda wondered if it was from the work . . . or from the parasite curled at the base of his neck. He understood why Meilin was pushing them so hard. They were running out of time.

"Thanks," Conor mumbled. "I could use a break."

"Are you sure it's real rockweed?" Meilin asked as she continued to scrape away at the gourd. "I wouldn't put it past Kovo to feed us something poisonous."

Takoda shook his head. "Will you ever learn to trust him?"

"No," Meilin said, her voice curt.

Takoda started to laugh, then stopped when he realized that Meilin was serious. He took some of the ropy plant and placed it in his mouth. "It's rockweed," he said as he chewed. "That I am positive of."

"Good. We'll need to gather as much as we can for the trip." Meilin dropped the stone that she had been using to clean the gourd and flexed her hands. They were red and raw from all the work. "What do you think, Conor?" she asked. "Good enough?"

After he didn't answer, Briggan nudged the boy with his nose.

Conor blinked, then looked from the wolf to Meilin. "Sorry. What were you saying?"

"Nothing important," she said. Meilin closed her eyes, touched the tattoo on the back of her hand, and grimaced. A few long seconds later, Jhi appeared. "Why don't you get some rest? Jhi will help with the infection while Takoda and I finish gathering the supplies for the trip. We can leave once we return."

Takoda's heartbeat sped up. He spat the rockweed from his mouth. "So soon? Maybe you should rest, too. Kovo and I can take the first watch—"

"No way," Meilin snapped.

"Even if you don't trust Kovo, you can trust me." He rustled the green cloak around his shoulders. "Don't forget, we're on the same side."

Jhi, who had been attending to Conor, now paused to watch the exchange between Takoda and Meilin. Her black ears twitched as she sat down, her heavy body settling softly into the sand. She leaned over to give Conor's skin another lick with her tongue, but her gaze remained on Takoda.

"It's not that I don't trust you," Meilin said. "It's just

that we're running out of time." She circled their make-shift boat so she was standing in front of Takoda. "And waiting an extra day won't bring her back."

As direct as she was, Meilin might as well have shoved a knife into his heart. "How do you know?" Takoda asked heatedly. He could hear the anger in his voice. The monks would have been displeased. "Xanthe knows these caves better than any of us. She'll eventually find her way to us."

"Takoda." Meilin's voice was soft, which just made Takoda more upset. "It's been at least two days. She would have found us by now, if she could." She looked across the sea. "Official Greencloak or not, you have a duty to save Sadre *for* Xanthe. It's what she would want."

Takoda wondered if there would even be anyone left in Sadre to save. So many had already fallen to the Wyrm and its parasites.

"Help me gather some materials for the trip," she said, placing her hand on his shoulder. "We still need something to use as a paddle."

He shook her hand off. "I don't know if I could ever be an *official* Greencloak, if it means becoming this cold. I suppose the great Meilin of Zhong must not know how it feels to lose someone important to her."

Meilin's eyes widened, then narrowed just as quickly. "Fine. Stay here and feel sorry for yourself. I'll gather the materials on my own." She turned and stormed up the beach.

Takoda watched her disappear into a cave. There was a bitter taste in his mouth that had little to do with the rockweed.

He caught sight of Jhi, still staring at him. Their eyes locked, and Takoda felt her enter his mind. Slowly, everything fueling his anger began to fade away. The ache in his stomach from hunger, the sadness from losing Xanthe and his parents, and even the hopelessness of their mission all dulled inside him.

After Takoda's heart had returned to a normal pace, Jhi released him. Then she looked toward the cave where Meilin had disappeared.

Takoda blew out a deep breath, then circled the gourd and approached Jhi and Conor. The anger that had filled Takoda before was now replaced with shame. "Thank you, Jhi," he said, kneeling in front of her. "Conor, do you think Jhi wants me to go after Meilin?"

"Better let her calm down first," Conor said. He gave Jhi a few pats on the head, right between her ears. "But *you* can follow Meilin if you want," he said to the panda. Jhi looked at Conor and tilted her head. "It's okay," Conor continued. "We both know that there isn't much more you can do for me, anyways."

Jhi gave him one last lick across the face, then ambled across the beach toward Meilin. Using the edge of the gourd as a brace, Conor rose from the ground, but he struggled to gain his footing in the sand.

"Let me help," Takoda said, jumping to his feet. He took Conor's arm and flung it over his shoulder, and pretended not to notice the parasite wiggling above Conor's collarbone.

They walked to the base of the cliffs, where they had set up a makeshift camp.

The cliffs stretched so high that it was impossible to

tell where they ended and the top of the large cavern began. They had fallen from up above, somewhere, in their rush to escape the burning fields.

The last time Takoda had seen Xanthe, her eyes were wide as she waved at them, trying to warn them to stop. Then, at the last second, she leaped out of the way as he, Conor, and Kovo crashed into Meilin and went tumbling over the ledge.

Once at camp, Conor sank into the sand and unfastened his cloak. "Meilin can be a little stubborn, but she means well. There's no one else you'd want with you in a battle."

Briggan lay down beside Conor and placed his muzzle in the boy's lap.

"I mean, after Briggan, of course." The animal seemed to grin at this.

"If you thought Meilin was mad a minute ago, you should have seen her when I suggested that you all leave me behind," Conor continued. "I thought she was going to punch me."

"I have much to learn about her," Takoda said. "About people in general. The monks in Nilo were not as . . . spirited as she is."

"I'll talk to her when she returns. Meilin doesn't want to admit it, but she needs rest as much as any of us." Conor sighed. "But she's right about Xanthe. We can't wait for her. We have to keep moving."

Takoda turned toward the sea. If Xanthe was out there, would she see their camp? Or was it too hidden from view?

"Her father," Conor said.

Takoda snapped back around. "What?"

"Meilin lost her father during the war. The war that Kovo started." Conor patted Briggan's flank. "I was there when General Teng died. The Devourer's crocodile killed him. I watched Meilin as she cried over his body," Conor said. "Then she stood up, wiped her eyes, and returned to her duty." Conor lay down beside Briggan. "She knows about loss, Takoda. More than any of us."

"What happened to her mother?" Takoda asked. Was she a warrior, too? Had she died during the war, like his mother had?

"She died a long time ago. I don't know the details." Conor yawned. "Sorry, I just need to rest for a little while. It's taking everything I have to fight..."

"To fight the parasite?" Takoda finished.

"No. To fight the Wyrm." Conor glanced at Takoda through lidded eyes. "I can feel it. The closer we get to it, the louder it becomes in my head. Like it's pulling me to it."

Takoda watched as Conor closed his eyes. "Does sleep help?" he asked.

"A little," Conor replied. "For now."

Takoda wasn't sure how much time Meilin and Jhi spent exploring the caves. Their time on the beach usually seemed to crawl by at a tortoise's pace, but with all the chores Takoda had completed while she was gone, he finally stopped counting the seconds.

Takoda didn't actually notice their return at first. It was Kovo who alerted him to it. The Great Ape sniffed the air, then made a clawing gesture over his face. *Cranky*. It was what he called Meilin.

A few seconds later, Meilin and her spirit animal came into view. "I didn't find much," Meilin said once she reached camp. "A little rockweed, and some vines we can use as a rope."

Takoda nodded toward the stick in her hand. "And a new quarterstaff?"

She shrugged. "It's not as long as I'd like, but it will come in handy if we're attacked from the water."

"Kovo and I went out as well. We gathered some rockweed, and even found a few of these." He moved his cloak, showing off two small spheres. "They aren't as bright as Xanthe's glowstones, but they will help us to preserve our last wooden torch." Takoda covered the orbs, then dragged a large mushroom stalk into his lap.

"What is that?" Meilin asked.

"Our oar," Takoda replied. "I found it while scavenging the shore. Kovo helped me break off the mushroom cap and drag the stalk here. Its fibers are strong—almost like wood—but I think I can sand it down enough to make a handle."

She was already shaking her head. "It's much too big to use."

"For us," Takoda said. "But not for Kovo."

Meilin pressed her lips together as she stared at the Great Beast. Kovo stared back, his eyes like red pinholes against his black fur. Meilin brushed her hair from her face. "I suppose we don't have much choice."

Takoda rose to his feet and leaned against the half-made paddle. "Sleep. I'll stand watch while I finish sanding this down."

"No, I'm—"

"I'm not only suggesting this for your benefit, or because I want to stay on the beach." Takoda glanced at Conor. Jhi had already returned to the boy's side. "Conor could use as much rest as we can allow. I promise we'll leave as soon as you both wake up. I won't fight you about it." Takoda waited for Meilin to sit down, then added, "And I'm sorry for what I said earlier. I shouldn't have been so careless with my words. Anyone who's faced as many battles as you have was sure to lose loved ones."

"I guess Conor told you about my father." She shook her head and gave off a mix of a snort and a huff. "He talks too much."

"Or perhaps you don't talk enough."

Meilin unfastened her cloak and folded it to use as a pillow. "There's an ancient Zhongese saying: The time of the bamboo flowering comes to us all. It's the life we lead that matters."

"The monks have a similar saying," Takoda said. "It's not the size of the pebble dropped into a pond that defines our impact on the world—but the ripples that remain in its wake." He picked up the stone he had been using to shape the oar. "My parents died during the war, too. My mother was a warrior. She died defending Nilo from the Conquerors. My father died while buying me time to escape."

Meilin blinked at Takoda, her face full of surprise. "I never knew that," she said softly.

Takoda shrugged. "Perhaps I don't talk enough, either."

Meilin glanced at Kovo. The ape had turned from Meilin and was instead looking out at the sea. "How can you stand being bonded to him, knowing what he did? What he was responsible for?"

"When I first called him, I wondered the same thing," Takoda said. "But the bond actually helps me to deal with the anger. Well, at least it *did*, until Xanthe . . ." He turned from Meilin because he didn't want her to see that his eyes were beginning to water. "Kovo isn't evil. Not really. He just sees himself as the best protector of Erdas."

"By starting two wars?" Meilin mumbled. "Yeah, that's a great way to show your love for Erdas."

Takoda finally laughed. "You should get some rest. I'll see you in a few hours."

Takoda walked away, dragging the stalk along with him. Kovo followed a few steps behind. Then Takoda stopped halfway across the beach and sank into the sand. He knew his hands would be just as red and raw as Meilin's once he finished with the oar. It was a small price to pay, given the gravity of their mission.

Kovo gently pushed Takoda's shoulder, then pointed toward the spot where Takoda usually sat.

Takoda shook his head. "I don't have time to waste, looking out at the sea. There's too much to do before Meilin and Conor wake up. And they're right. There's nothing more I can do for Xanthe." He swallowed the lump in his throat. "She was the pebble. We must be the ripples."

Kovo knelt in front of Takoda. His eyes were so large. So red. But not angry—at least, not right then. Kovo grunted, then closed his hand into a fist and made a small circle motion across his chest.

Takoda sat up. "You're ... *sorry*?" he asked. Kovo had never used that word before. "I didn't think you even liked Xanthe."

Kovo pointed to Takoda, then placed his two pointer fingers together. Kovo followed this gesture by bringing his open hands down in front of his face.

"Yes, I'm hurt," Takoda said. "And very sad." Takoda could hardly believe the conversation that he was having with Kovo. Takoda had always assumed that the ape saw him as a necessary nuisance. Was it possible that Kovo actually *cared* for him?

He studied Kovo's face, looking for the arrogance and contempt that usually resided there. Finding none of that, he took his hand, placed it against his lips, then brought it down to his lap. "Thank you, Kovo." Then he formed a fist and slowly repeated the gesture that the Great Beast had just made. "And ... I'm sorry, too."

DANTE

S TANDING ABOARD THE *TELLUN'S PRIDE II*, ABEKE'S HEART swelled as she stared at the sand-colored rocky cliffs in the distance. Nilo. Home. Although the busy port towns along the northern border were very different from Okaihee, the idea of being on familiar ground made her ache for the savannah.

Abeke looked up at the sunny sky and floating clouds. The winds blew in their favor, filling the ship's sails and pushing them that much closer to Nilo. The *Tellun's Pride II* was not meant to be manned by a crew of three, but she, Rollan, and Tasha were making do. She and Rollan had traveled on enough ships in their short time as Greencloaks to understand how to hoist the sails, secure the decks, and steer the ship. They'd found the waters tucked between Nilo and Eura were much calmer than the open sea. Almost pleasant. Out of all of them, it was only Uraza that seemed bothered by the constant, buoyant rhythm of the ship.

Uraza remained still as Abeke reached down and

petted her flank. She knew the leopard would rather be in passive state than walking around the boat. The Great Beast had spent the entire trip moaning and growling, her strong legs unsure on the wooden planks. But Abeke couldn't bring herself to call Uraza to her passive state. Abeke could still feel the effects of the last bond-breaking incident. It had felt like her skin—her bones—had been ablaze. And afterward, there was so much silence between her and Uraza. So much distance. She could hardly feel Uraza now. And what if Uraza was in her passive state when the bonds completely severed? What would happen to them both?

Suddenly, Abeke found herself thinking of the Greencloaks who had been infected. What had happened to their spirit animals? And what of Conor and Briggan? Was he still fighting the infection, or had he turned into a mindless slave like so many others?

"I'm sorry," Abeke said to Uraza. She put her face close to the leopard's nose. "I know you're uncomfortable, but I can't take the chance of losing you permanently."

Abeke looked up as a shadow approached.

"Am I interrupting something?" Rollan asked with a grin on his face. He'd been trying to keep the mood light, always ready with a new joke or story—most of them dreadfully painful. But today was the first time that she'd seen Tasha smile since their escape from Stetriol. They all deserved a bit of joy before their next mission.

"Don't be jealous just because Uraza and I are closer than you and Essix," Abeke said, with a hint of laughter in her voice.

"Hey, Essix and I have a great relationship. She stays out of my way, and I stay out of hers." Rollan's chest swelled as he looked up. "She knows where to find me when she needs me."

"When she needs *you*?"

"Okay, okay." Rollan shrugged. "Maybe it's the other way around."

"You're both loners at heart." Abeke patted Uraza one last time before rising to her feet. "Does that make it . . . easier?"

Rollan took a deep breath. Abeke knew she didn't have to explain what she was trying to ask. "We've always been more distant," he said. "If something happened with the bonds and they actually broke, I think she'd be okay without me." Rollan flapped his green cloak. "And who's a loner now?"

Abeke noticed that he didn't say how *he* would fare without Essix. "And how is Tasha?"

"Better. She went downstairs to change. I guess she doesn't want to arrive in Caylif smelling of sardines and cabbage." Unlike Abeke and Rollan, Tasha had eventually begun sleeping in the captain's quarters belowdecks. For Abeke, it reminded her too much of Nisha, Arac, and all the other Greencloaks who had been lost to Zerif's parasites on Stetriol.

"I'd hoped that Lenori would send another message, or even Greenhaven," Abeke said. They had only received two missives since departing Stetriol—one telling them that Greenhaven had fallen to Zerif, and the second directing them to a small fishing village west of Caylif. They were to rendezvous with Dante, a former Greencloak.

"According to Essix, we should be arriving soon," Rollan said. "Let's hope this Dante knows where to find Cabaro."

"Do you think we're doing the right thing?" Abeke asked. "Maybe we should go to Greenhaven anyway. Surely there's something we could do to help our friends."

"Believe me, if circumstances were different, I'd easily pick a fight with Zerif over Cabaro," Rollan replied. "But remember how tough he was in Amaya? Now think about how difficult it would be to face him with a castle full of Greencloaks and spirit animals on his side. We don't want to give him the opportunity to steal more Great Beasts."

Abeke nodded. "I suppose you're right." Rollan turned to walk away, but Abeke motioned for him to stop. "Something you just said—you expect a fight with Cabaro? We didn't have any resistance from Tellun or Ninani."

"Tellun and Ninani have always been on the Greencloaks' side," Rollan said. "Cabaro hates humans."

"Maybe he has no choice but to accept humans, now that he's bonded with one."

Rollan's hands tightened around his cloak. "Or maybe that'll give him reason to hate us more."

A few hours later, the *Tellun's Pride II* drew into a small natural bay. Abeke, Rollan, and Tasha worked together to lower the sails and drop the anchor in the calm, deep blue waters. They thought it would be safer to take a smaller skiff in than to try to navigate the large ship farther into the harbor.

They gathered on the deck and looked out at the small village. It was silent—Abeke couldn't even hear the calls of wild animals. A few withered and fragile piers jutted from the mainland out into the water. A lone man stood on one of the docks, but he was too far away for Abeke to determine much about him. All Abeke could tell was that he wasn't wearing a cloak.

"Is that the person we're looking for?" Tasha asked. "Do you want me to climb to the crow's nest to get a better look?"

"No need," Rollan said. A few seconds later, his eyes went glassy. Up above, Essix soared past, toward the man on the pier.

"Do you think I'll be able to do that with Ninani one day?" Tasha asked. "See through her eyes like Rollan does with Essix?"

It was when Tasha began asking questions that Abeke missed the adult Greencloaks the most. Tasha looked to Abeke and Rollan as if they were experts on all things related to spirit animals. The truth was, both she and Rollan still had much to learn about their own bonds. But Abeke also knew that Tasha needed to believe someone was in charge, even though Abeke wasn't exactly sure that she and Rollan really knew what they were doing.

"Each spirit animal brings different gifts, as I'm sure you've already discovered," Abeke finally said. "I'd bet that you move much faster with her helping you. Your reflexes are also sharper, correct?"

"Ninani makes me much more graceful—I'm all left feet without her."

"All left feet?" Abeke repeated.

"Just slang from back home," Tasha said. "It means that I'm clumsy." She pointed to her boots, which she'd found in an abandoned trunk belowdecks. "You know, like I have two left feet instead of a left and a right one."

Abeke grinned. "Ninani's grace will certainly help with that. And there could be even more gifts that you'll discover in time. The Greencloaks will help teach you."

If any Greencloaks remain, Abeke thought.

Rollan shook his head as his eyes returned to normal. He leaned against the rail and took in a few deep breaths. Even though he didn't want to admit it to her, Abeke could tell that the loosening bonds between humans and their spirit animals were affecting Rollan, too. "That could be Dante," he said after he caught his breath. "It's hard to tell. I didn't see any spirit animal beside him, but it could just be in passive state."

"I guess there's only one way to find out," Abeke said.

Rollan slowly climbed into the docking boat, then Tasha. Abeke started to climb in as well, until she noticed her spirit animal hanging back.

"Uraza," Abeke called out. "Please."

"You know, maybe it makes sense for someone to stay here and guard the ship," Rollan said. "Tasha and I can check things out at the pier."

Abeke shook her head. "Without knowing what lies ahead, we're better off staying together." She closed her eyes, cleared her mind, then called Uraza to her. A second later, the Great Beast disappeared with a hot flash onto a small black mark below her elbow.

The trip to the harbor took less time than Abeke would have liked. While Rollan and Tasha rowed, she held her bow low, the arrow already nocked. With everything else happening in Erdas, they couldn't take any chances.

The man walked to the end of the pier as they approached. Rollan and Tasha stopped rowing. "Identify yourself," Abeke called out. She raised her bow, just enough to make sure he saw the arrow.

The man was tall, with broad shoulders, tanned skin, and high cheekbones. His face was clean-shaven, and his long hair was pulled into a thick ponytail. Abeke couldn't tell where he was from by looking at him, but she was sure that he wasn't a native Niloan.

"I am Dante," he said, offering a small bow. "At your service. And you are Abeke and Rollan. And your friend . . . are you the one who called Ninani?"

"If you're really Dante, you would be wearing your cloak." Rollan placed his hand on the hilt of the knife tucked into his waistband. "Try again."

"Ah, yes, you are most definitely Rollan. Lenori has spoken much of you." He pulled a small, rolled note from his hand. "You probably have no idea of how proud you made all of Amaya during the war. You and Essix are national heroes."

As if on cue, Essix swooped down from the sky and landed on Dante's shoulder. Dante stretched out his hand, offering up the note to the gyrfalcon. Essix gingerly picked up the parchment with her beak, then flew to Rollan.

Rollan unfurled the note and read it, while Essix

rested on his shoulder. "It looks like Lenori's hand-writing," he whispered. "And clearly Essix trusts him."

Dante opened his backpack and pulled out a faded green cloak. "Permission to come aboard?"

There was one thing for certain—Dante knew his way around a ship. He worked twice as fast as Abeke, Rollan, and Tasha combined. And when Tasha knocked over a large barrel, almost smashing his foot, he didn't yell at her. Instead, he calmly showed her a better knot to use to tie down the cargo.

After they had pulled out of the bay, they all met at the ship's wheel. "We may be cutting it close, but I think we can make it to Caylif before dusk," Dante said.

"And this is where we'll find Cabaro?" Tasha asked.

Dante nodded. "Cabaro was summoned by a boy named Kirat. His father, Faisel, is one of the wealthiest merchants in Nilo. Some estimate that he controls a third of the trade routes between Northern Nilo and Zhong. Honestly, I'm surprised that word of Cabaro's summoning hadn't reached Stetriol. Faisel has been telling everyone about the lion and has even planned a feast in honor of Cabaro and his son."

Abeke thought back to their time in Stetriol—how Zerif's forces had arrived as word of Ninani's appearance spread. If word of Cabaro had spread similarly . . .

"We have to move quickly," she said. "We must contact Faisel at once."

"I've tried," Dante said. "Once this latest crisis began, Lenori coaxed me out of retirement. I was on my way to

Greenhaven when she sent word asking me to stop here and warn Faisel." He rubbed his hands together. "Faisel hasn't been willing to meet with me. He feels that he has no need for our help."

"Yeah, well, he hasn't seen what Zerif can do," Rollan said.

"And Zerif hasn't seen Zourtzi," Dante countered.

Tasha frowned. "What's Zourtzi?"

Dante smiled. "You will see it soon enough for yourself. It's just around the bend."

Tasha turned to Dante. "And what's your spirit animal?" she asked.

As Dante frowned, Tasha brought her hand to her mouth. "I'm sorry. Should I not have asked?"

"It's okay," Dante said. He raised his sleeve and rubbed a pale spot on his wrist. "Aputin was my spirit animal. The finest mountain goat ever seen." He rolled his sleeve back down. "He was killed during the war. It was like losing an arm. No, it was worse."

No one spoke for a few seconds. Finally, Tasha said, "I'm sorry."

"Many of us paid a large price during the war." He rearranged his cloak on his shoulders. "But whether I have Aputin by my side or not, I will always be a Greencloak."

"What does it mean?" Abeke asked. "Aputin?"

"It's a type of rock, isn't it?" Rollan asked.

"Not just any rock," Dante said. "It's one of the hardest minerals found in Amaya. Very difficult to cut or shape." Dante smiled. "It seemed like a fitting name for a spirit animal that liked to head-butt me when we disagreed." Dante looked at the others. "I guess you all didn't have to worry about naming your partners."

Abeke rubbed the mark on her arm. While she was honored to have called forth Uraza, she sometimes wondered what she would have named her spirit animal if she had bonded with another creature instead of one of the Great Beasts. She knew that Tarik, their former guardian, had named his spirit animal Lumeo, which meant "light." It fit the otter's playful, clownish nature. And Hano, a boy from her village, had named his anteater Digger because of the way the animal burrowed into the ground with its long snout and sharp claws. Would Abeke have picked a name based on Uraza's nature? Or would she have named the animal after her mother, like she had sometimes dreamed?

A few minutes later, a large stone fortress came into view. Abeke had never seen a structure so tall—it was three times the size of Greenhaven. Large bronze cannons stood at the top of every tower. Even from far away, Abeke could see the sentries at each of the battlements.

"That, my young friends, is Zourtzi. It has been in Faisel's family for generations. The rumor is that its walls have never been breached, even during both of the Devourer wars." Dante pointed to toward the castle. "Save for a small man-made channel, the island fortress is surrounded by a network of shallow, rocky reefs. It makes a water approach nearly impossible, and it also pushes most ships' cannons out of range."

"What is it made of?" Tasha asked. "The walls look so . . . smooth."

"It's built from solid stone imported from Zhong," Dante said. "Once the outer wall was completed, each brick was sanded down to make it flush with the mortar. There is no way any animal could scale that wall, much less a human."

"Unnavigable water and unclimbable walls," Rollan muttered. "I'm guessing this Faisel guy isn't too keen on people popping in to say hello."

"I've tried to contact Faisel every way I know how. But perhaps he will listen to the Heroes of Erdas," Dante said.

Out of the corner of her eye, Abeke saw Rollan frown. She knew how much he hated being called a hero. "Perhaps we could—what's that sound?"

They all looked around as a whistle grew louder. Abeke wasn't sure, but it seemed to be coming from above.

"Take cover!" Dante yelled. "We're under attack!"

Just then, a cannonball splashed into the water, drenching the deck with seawater.

Abeke scrambled to the bridge and jerked the wheel, steering the ship away from the fortress. "Everyone okay?" she asked.

Tasha looked even paler than usual as she huddled against the rail, but she nodded. "I'm fine," she said, in rushed, ragged breaths. Her braid had come undone when she'd ducked, causing her fine, blond hair to spill across her face.

Rollan pushed himself to his feet and winced as he rubbed his shoulder. "I thought you said that it was too far for cannons to fire?" he mumbled.

"Too far for a *ship's* cannons," Dante said. "Not Zourtzi's. The additional height of the fortress increases their cannons' range."

"So now what?" Rollan asked. "We're sitting ducks out here."

Abeke shook her head. "The cannonball landed too far away. I don't think they were actually trying to attack us."

"I agree," Dante said. He shielded his eyes from the sun and gazed at the fortress. "It was a warning shot."

Rollan snorted. "Message received, loud and clear."

The sun was just beginning to set as the *Tellun's Pride II* reached Caylif. Hints of orange, red, and yellow danced along the waterline, reminding Abeke yet again of the plains surrounding her village.

Abeke watched as Dante steered the large vessel into the bay. It was nothing like the fishing village where they had found him—or anywhere else she had been for that matter. Even as evening approached, the docks swarmed with deckhands and merchants. Dante had asked Abeke to drop all the sails except one, using it to slowly maneuver the ship through the docks. He motioned for her to drop the last sail as Rollan tossed a set of ropes to a group of men on the pier. They slowly winched the ship into place, then tied it off on a large wooden bollard.

"Okay, so I have to admit, he has his perks," Rollan said as Dante tossed the men on the pier a few coins.

"I don't think we would have been able to get the ship into the dock without him."

"It *is* good to have someone else around," Abeke said. "Someone older."

"Yeah. It's like it doesn't feel so hard—so impossible—with Dante here. It's almost like . . ." Rollan cleared his throat. "It's almost like it was when Tarik traveled with us."

Abeke let the silence linger between them. Much time had passed since their guardian had fallen in battle, but for Rollan it was a wound that still ran deep.

"Are we going into town?" Tasha asked as she exited the ship's galley. It had been her turn to prepare the meal—not that there was much variety to choose from. They had eaten sardines and pickled cabbage every day since escaping from Stetriol. It was the only food remaining on the ship.

"It would be best to wait until tomorrow," Dante answered as he joined them. "The market will be closing soon. And the man we need to see probably isn't there at this hour, anyway." Then Dante sniffed the air. "Are those pickled cabbages?"

Tasha nodded. "It's all we have left. That, and sardines."

"And how are you preparing them?" he asked, drawing in another deep breath. "Are you *boiling* them?"

"How else are you supposed to cook them?" Tasha asked.

Dante turned to Rollan for help. "Seriously, is that how you all prepare your food?"

Rollan shrugged. "I just eat them raw. Saves time."

"Tasha, go through my bag and pull out the small package of red and black seasoning." Dante shook his head and rolled up his sleeves. "Boiled cabbage. What are you all, savages?"

Tasha retrieved the spices, then Dante entered the galley.

When he returned an hour later, he carried a large, heaping plate of food. "I call it Dante's Stir-Fried Cabbage Surprise." He handed the plate to Rollan. "Just a little something I picked up from a cook while I was stationed at the Mire. Enjoy."

"You were at the Mire? In Zhong?" Abeke asked. She had overheard others speaking of the Mire, a Greencloak prison deep in the jungle in Southern Zhong. It was reserved for the most dangerous criminals.

"Yeah. I served as a guard there. Twice." A small smile spread across Dante's lips as he cracked his knuckles. "Aputin and I were very good at . . . keeping prisoners in line."

Abeke shuddered as she took the plate from Rollan. As nice as Dante was, there was something dark just below the surface. While Tarik had often wanted to avoid conflict, she got the sense that Dante enjoyed battle.

Tasha scooped some of the food into a bowl next. "Where are the sardines?" she asked.

"They're in there," Dante said. "I just chopped them up. They're less salty that way."

Rollan had already shoveled three spoonfuls of food into his mouth. "This is amazing!"

"I wish I could take credit, but it's all in the spices," Dante said.

"And do you always carry a package of spices with you?" Abeke asked. "Did you pick that up while in the Mire as well?"

Dante shook his head. "Those aren't Zhongese spices. They're native to my home in Amaya. Sanabajari."

Rollan glanced at Abeke. "Why does that name sound familiar?"

"You may know it by a different name," Dante said, smiling. "Boulder City."

Rollan's eyes lit up. "Do you know Monte? Is he still running his trading post?"

Abeke noticed the confusion on Tasha's face. "Monte is an old friend," Abeke said. "We met him during one of our first battles." Abeke decided not to tell Tasha that she had actually been fighting on the enemies' side back then. But at the time, Abeke hadn't known that Shane and Zerif were evil. She hadn't discovered that until Zerif plunged his knife into a defenseless Greencloak's back.

"No, Monte's given up the trading post," Dante said. "I was tending it for him, until Lenori convinced me to come back." Dante spooned some food into his mouth. "I had been looking forward to seeing Monte again. It's been too long. His regulars are starting to miss him."

"Where is he now?" Tasha asked. "Off on another mission?"

Dante's face soured. "No. He was in Greenhaven, along with the others."

Tasha took a deep breath. "I'm sorry–"

"There's nothing to apologize for," Dante said. "There is never any harm in asking a question. You just have to be prepared to hear the answer."

Silence followed, while Tasha took this in. Her eyes fell to her hands. Finally, she rose from the deck. "In that case, I think I've asked enough questions for tonight," she said with a weak smile. "I'll see you all tomorrow morning."

Abeke watched her disappear belowdecks. "She is so green. I hope she's ready for what lies ahead."

"Were any of us really ready when we first received the call? When we first fastened the cloak around our shoulders?" Dante scooped more food into his bowl. "If she's going to fight among the Greencloaks, she must learn that this life isn't for the faint of heart. And believe me, it's best for her to learn this sooner rather than later."

THE MARKET

ROLLAN WALKED A FEW STEPS AHEAD OF DANTE, ABEKE, and Tasha as they neared the large market in the center of town. He hadn't expected to feel so apprehensive. He had grown up in a large city just like Caylif—out of all of them, he should have felt the most at ease. Yet even as the familiar sounds of the market began to fill his ears—women selling handmade pots, boys hawking fresh fruit, and men counting gold coins—Rollan still felt on edge.

He looked overhead as Essix soared past. She had come to the ship as soon as they docked yesterday evening and had remained through the entire night. He was glad to have her nearby. Unlike the others, the gyrfalcon understood exactly what lay ahead.

Abeke hadn't been with him and Conor when they had first faced Cabaro, here in Nilo. The Great Beast hadn't fought them initially, instead allowing his lionesses to do his dirty work. When Cabaro finally struck, he was ferocious, almost crushing Briggan during the fight. But when the Conquerors arrived to take his talisman, Cabaro did what he did best. He retreated.

It was during his escape that Cabaro had almost trampled Rollan. Rollan could still remember Cabaro's foot coming toward him—his claws were as large as Rollan's body. The Great Lion would have crushed him if Tarik hadn't pulled him out of the way.

Tarik . . .

"What's wrong, Rollan?" Abeke asked.

Rollan blinked. He hadn't even heard Abeke creep up behind him. "What makes you think something's wrong?" he asked.

"You haven't told a joke since we left the ship," she replied. "And you hardly ate your breakfast."

"First of all, I wouldn't call leftover cabbage a proper breakfast," he said "And don't worry about the jokes. I'm saving them all up for Faisel. Maybe a little humor and charm is all we need to convince him to let us steal his prized son away."

"I wouldn't call him prized," Abeke said. "According to Dante, Faisel and his son have a difficult relationship." She sighed. "Perhaps that's one thing he and I will have in common." Then she patted Rollan's shoulder. "I know you're worried about Cabaro joining us because we're humans. But surely even he will understand the importance of what we're trying to do. His fate is tied to Erdas, just as ours is."

Rollan shrugged. He wouldn't admit it to Abeke—he could hardly admit it to himself—but that wasn't the only reason he was feeling squeamish. The fact that they were here to rescue the Great Lion was drumming up some not-so-great memories.

Rollan touched his cloak. *Tarik's* cloak. Abeke and Faisel's son had difficult relationships with their fathers, but at least they *had* fathers. Tarik was the closest person to a father he'd ever had. And thanks to the cowardly Cabaro—

No. Rollan couldn't let himself think about Tarik now. Too much was at stake. He had to remain sharp. Focused. Tarik would have told him just as much if he had been there.

Rollan paused at the edge of the market and waited for Dante and Tasha to catch up. The market looked even larger than the main market in his hometown of Concorba. Large multicolored tents billowed in the breeze, and white smoke from the cooking pits filled the air. People pushed and jostled each other as they made their way from merchant to merchant. He could hear at least three different languages, if not more.

He grinned. This was a thief's paradise.

Not that he stole things anymore, but a boy could dream.

Finally, Dante and Tasha joined them. Tasha was the slowest of the group, but Rollan hadn't once heard Dante chastise her for it. She was carrying a wooden baton that she had found in the armory, but the weapon looked out of place in her hands.

"So now what?" Rollan asked. "Should we just walk around until we find his shop?"

"And how long will that take?" Abeke asked. "My entire village could fit inside this market."

Rollan spotted a small kid huddled in the corner, chewing on a thick slice of bread. The boy's clothes were much too big for him, and his face was streaked with red dirt. "Hey, kid," he called. Once the boy looked up, Rollan pulled a small coin from his pocket. The boy perked up and ran over to them.

Rollan dropped the coin into the boy's hand. "We're looking for a shop belonging to a merchant named Faisel."

After staring at the coin for a few seconds, the boy looked at Rollan. "Which shop? Faisel owns a silk shop, a carpet store, a cart for selling spices, a–"

"What about Otto?" Dante asked. "The large, round man with a gray beard. Where can we find him?"

"Hold on. Let me check." The boy ran to a group of kids huddled around a well. After speaking in whispered tones, he returned to Rollan. "We think he's at the silk shop today." The boy pocketed the coin and pointed. "It's on the eastern side of the market."

Rollan flashed another coin. "How about you lead us there, and you can add this to your collection?"

The boy nodded, and the others fell into step behind him.

"Who is Otto?" Tasha asked.

"He's one of Faisel's business partners," Dante said. "If we impress him enough–and pay him enough–he should be able to grant us an audience with Faisel. But I should warn you, Otto and I have spoken of this before. It didn't end well–for him."

As the group made their way through the market, Rollan noticed a lot of people were staring at them.

"Should we take off our cloaks?" he whispered. "We're drawing a lot of attention to ourselves."

"No, that's exactly what we want," Dante said. "The more important we seem, the more we will impress Otto." He glanced at Rollan. "When the time comes, we will need Essix."

Rollan nodded. "She'll be there."

At least Rollan hoped she'd be there. He and Essix had always been comfortable working independently of each other, going long stretches of time without direct contact, but even *they* weren't immune to the effects of the bond loosening. It took so much effort for Rollan to see through her eyes, and he could only do it in spurts. Almost every time afterward, he felt sick to his stomach, as if he'd drunk a bowl of spoiled milk.

Even now, the bond between them was so faint. He knew that Essix was somewhere above, but that was all he knew. She could have been ten paces away or a hundred. Or a thousand. He could no longer tell the difference.

They had to stop Zerif and fix the Evertree. Rollan had already lost so many others. He couldn't lose Essix, too.

Rollan flipped the coin to the boy when they reached the shop. "Be sure to share that with your friends," Rollan said. He hoped those coins would buy a few loaves of bread and blocks of cheese.

The silk shop, with its gold trim and large, flowing flags, was clearly designed to draw attention to itself. Rollan wouldn't have dared to even approach a store like this when he was living on the street. He would have been thrown in jail or sent to an orphanage for just *thinking* about entering such a fine shop.

And even though he could now afford to shop here, he still didn't feel as if he belonged. Maybe he never would.

Dante entered the shop first, ringing a small bell hanging in the doorway. Rollan was the last to enter. As he shut the door behind him, the noises and smells of the market faded away.

"Beautiful," Tasha said as she ran her hands along a row of colored silk ribbons.

Rollan picked up a dark red silk scarf. Something about it reminded him of Meilin. He hoped she was safe, wherever she was. Lenori hadn't sent any additional word of her or Conor. Rollan had been telling himself that no news was good news.

"Can I help you?" a young man asked, rushing up to the group. His black hair was slicked back, and his skin looked much too oily, considering the dry atmosphere. "Ah, Greencloaks," he said. "What can I do for such fine warriors? I'd be happy to show you our new shipment of silks and linens. Or maybe our handmade tunics."

Dante waved him off. "We're here to see Otto."

The young man faltered. "Mzee Otto is extremely busy. Are you sure there's not something I could help you with?"

Dante placed his hand on the hilt of his sword. "Don't make me repeat myself."

The young man nodded, then disappeared in the rear of the store. Abeke shook her head. "Was there not another way? I don't like intimidating people with violence."

"Says the girl who met me with a bow in her hand," Dante replied.

A few minutes later, a large, round man approached the group. Three men followed him, each dressed in black. A small snake had curled itself around one of the men's shoulders. A monkey hung around the neck of the other. The third didn't have a spirit animal in sight, but that didn't mean he wasn't one of the Marked.

"Dante, you've returned," the man said. "And you've brought reinforcements." He nodded toward the men behind him. "So did I."

Dante opened his hands, signaling for peace. "Otto, I know our last meeting didn't end on the best terms, but I wanted to give you another chance to arrange an audience with Faisel. I assure you, he would look at you most favorably."

"Faisel has no need for a has-been Greencloak and a bunch of kids."

If Dante was offended, he didn't show it. "These are not any ordinary children, Otto." He nodded toward Abeke. "If you don't mind . . ."

Abeke closed her eyes, scrunched her face, and finally Uraza appeared with a flash of light. Then Ninani.

Rollan cleared his throat. *Anytime, Essix.*

Finally, there was a shriek from an open window. Essix looked at Rollan, as if she were saying, *Told you I'd be here.*

"Don't you think it would be fitting for Cabaro to be reunited with the other Great Beasts?" Dante offered.

"They don't look very great to me," Otto said.

Rollan crossed his arms. "Bet you wouldn't say something like that to Cabaro."

Otto scowled at Rollan. "Boy, don't forget whose shop you're in!"

"Faisel's shop. Not yours," Dante said. "Exclude me if you must—but let my young friends enter Zourtzi and pay their respects to Faisel, Kirat, and Cabaro."

Rollan glanced at Abeke and Uraza out of the corner of his eye. They both looked restless. He pulled the bag of coins from his pocket. It was the last of their money, but getting them into Zourtzi would be worth the cost. "Listen to Dante. You could also profit greatly."

"How much is in that bag, boy?"

Rollan could hear the greed seeping from Otto's voice. "Take us to Faisel, and you can find out for yourself," Rollan replied.

"Do you think I need your coins?" Then Otto smirked. "Actually, I *will* take the money. Your presence alone has probably cost me an hour's worth of sales. Guards."

Dante drew his sword as the guard with the snake advanced. Dante's straight blade looked out of place against the curved swords of northern Nilo. "Otto, we do not want to fight," he said. "But if we can't pay you enough to take us to Faisel, perhaps we can persuade you in another way."

Rollan pulled out his dagger. "Tasha, get behind me," he whispered.

Tasha fiercely shook her head as she tightened her grip on her baton. "If you fight, then I will fight."

Great, Rollan thought. That sounded like something Meilin would say. Unfortunately, he knew Tasha didn't have the skills to back up her words.

Abeke had already pulled an arrow from her quiver, though she'd yet to draw her bow. "You all have spirit animals," she said to the men. "You've felt your bonds straining over the past few days, yes? Something is happening to the connection between humans and spirit animals. That's why we *must* find Cabaro. We need his help if we're going to stop this evil from destroying the world."

While two of the guards paused at this, the one with the snake charged forward. Dante blocked him, then kicked him in the chest. The man flew backward onto Otto. Even without the help of his spirit animal, Dante was still a gifted fighter.

"Watch out for the snake!" Abeke yelled. "It's on your arm."

Dante yelped as the snake's fangs pierced his sleeve. He shook it off, then kicked the snake across the room, where it disappeared into a pile of silk sheets.

"Dante, are you all right?" Rollan yelled, his voice almost in a scream. As Dante inspected his arm, Rollan replayed Tarik being struck by Gerathon the Serpent.

"Its fangs barely grazed my arm. I'll be fine," Dante said as he backed up beside Abeke. The two remaining guards were slowly approaching. The last guard had called his spirit animal, a lynx, which was already lunging at Uraza. "Look alive, Greencloaks!" Dante yelled.

Rollan didn't have much time to watch Dante and Abeke, as the man with the monkey had almost reached him and Tasha. The guard pulled an ax from his side and swung. Rollan ducked, easily dodging the ax's blade, then swiped his knife at the guard's stomach. Rollan missed, catching only the fabric of the guard's shirt. Before he could swing again, the guard's monkey leaped onto his face, shrieking and clawing with its hands.

Rollan dropped his dagger and tried to pry the animal off before it scratched his eyes out. Unable to remove it, he fell to the floor and began to roll around.

"Essix!" Rollan yelled.

Rollan sensed Essix taking flight. A few seconds later, the gyrfalcon had pulled the monkey from his neck and face. Then Essix flew off out the window with the monkey still in her talons.

"Bhouhan!" the man yelled as Essix and the monkey disappeared. Then the guard turned back to Tasha and Rollan with renewed determination in his eyes. Seeing Rollan still on the ground, he raised his ax high above his head. He quickly brought it down—and was blocked by Tasha's baton. Spinning in place, she forced the attacker back and placed herself in front of Rollan. "Are you okay?" she asked over her shoulder.

"I'm good. Thanks!" As Rollan got to his feet, he saw Ninani standing in the corner, her white wings splayed open. She must have been augmenting Tasha's grace. There was no way that Tasha could fight the guard on her own.

Rollan picked up his dagger. His skin burned where the monkey had scratched him. "Ready?" he called. "Together!"

He and Tasha ran toward the man at the same time. The guard swung again, but Tasha easily blocked his attack, allowing Rollan to bury his knife into the man's shoulder. The man screamed in pain and dropped his ax. He looked at the blood pouring from the wound and quickly retreated.

Rollan turned toward Abeke and was happy to see that she was holding the other guards at bay with her bow and arrow. One of their attackers had an arrow in his leg, and the other held his shoulder as if it were broken.

"Is everyone all right?" Abeke asked, not taking her eyes off the guards.

"Nothing a cold compress and bandage can't fix," Rollan said, wiping the blood away from his face. "Tasha?"

The girl shook her head as she stared at the end of the baton. There were nicks in the wood where it had blocked the ax blade. "I can't believe I just did all of that. I've never even used a weapon like this until today."

"Well, I'm glad you're a quick study," Rollan said. "We should also thank Ninani. I'm sure she had a lot to do with your newfound abilities."

Ninani waddled over to Tasha and rubbed the girl's leg with the crown of her head. "Will I ever get used to it? All this fighting?"

Rollan sighed. "Yes. But I suppose that isn't a good thing."

Abeke motioned for Rollan to join her. "I'll talk to Tasha and make sure she's okay," Abeke whispered to him. "Maybe you should check on Dante."

Rollan turned to see Dante standing over Otto, his sword at the large man's chin.

"Get up," Dante demanded.

"You idiot, you sliced my leg!" Otto wailed from his fetal position on the floor.

"At least I didn't break it." Dante poked Otto with his sword. "Now get up. You're taking us to see Faisel, even if I have to carry you there."

As Otto hobbled to his feet, Rollan heard a commotion outside the building. Suddenly, more guards burst through the back entrance, led by the young salesman from earlier. There were at least six men, with more pouring in. They started running toward them but were slowed down by the maze of silk racks.

"Head out the front!" Rollan yelled to Tasha and Abeke. He turned to Dante. "We have to go," he said. "And you have to leave Otto. He'll slow us down."

Dante sneered at Otto but turned and followed Rollan. Outside, two more guards were lying on their backs, moaning in pain. A third was pressed underneath Uraza's paw. Rollan glanced at Tasha, whose fingers were still tight around her baton. "Remind me never to get in a fight with you."

"So now what?" Tasha asked.

The yelling in the shop grew louder. "We run," Rollan said, taking off. He sped into a nearby alley, then slowed to make sure everyone had followed. Dante was holding his arm as he ran. The Greencloak had said that the snake had barely grazed his arm, that the injury wasn't that bad. But what if he was wrong?

Rollan continued down the alley, sprinting between merchants, shoppers, and carts. He passed the last large group of people, then slid to a halt. Now that the path was clear, he could see the large beige brick wall stretching before him. Even with the help of their spirit animal partners, Rollan didn't think they would be able to scale the wall. Certainly not before the guards reached them.

Abeke came to a stop beside Rollan. "Now what?" she asked. "Maybe we could hide in one of the carts."

"Over here!"

Rollan turned around and spotted their young guide from earlier. He was tucked behind two large potted plants. "Follow me!" the boy yelled, before disappearing behind the thick green leaves.

"Can we trust him?" Dante asked.

"I don't believe we have a choice." Abeke released an arrow as one of the guards entered the alley, then called Uraza into her dormant state. Rollan assumed that Tasha had done the same for Ninani, because the swan was nowhere in sight.

They pushed their way through the plants, revealing an even smaller alleyway between a high stone wall and a row of rickety wooden buildings. It was tight, especially for Dante and his broad shoulders, but they quickly inched their way through.

"We should have stayed and fought," Dante said. "We're Greencloaks."

"Us and what army?" Rollan quipped. "Just keep pushing ahead."

Rollan heard the guards behind him. They had reached the alleyway. He only hoped that they didn't have arrows.

"You stay here," one of the guards yelled. "I'll circle around and cut them off."

Rollan tried to judge how much farther they had until they reached the other side. They were moving, but not fast enough. *Now would be a really good time for one of those Redcloak guys to show up*, he thought.

Dante must have realized how slowly they were moving as well. "We'll never make it to the other side in time!"

"We're not going to the other side," their guide replied as he climbed–*into the wall?* Rollan reached the spot where the boy had disappeared. There was a large, jagged hole in the wall, opening up to a weathered rock ledge overlooking the entire city. In the valley below, hundreds of small huts and mud-brick shacks lined weaving streets. Then a wide river cut through the city, dividing it. Large white limestone homes sat on the opposite side of the river. Some houses looked big enough to comfortably hold every Greencloak in Greenhaven. Beyond those homes was the first in a series of mountains, their peaks hazy in the sun's orange glow. It was all breathtaking, for the few seconds that Rollan had to enjoy it.

"This way," the boy called as he inched along the wall. "But watch your step."

Rollan's feet barely fit on the ledge. He slowly followed the boy and tried not to look down.

"We're almost there," the boy said. "There's a sinkhole up ahead. It drops down into a natural well. The water should be deep enough for you to fall through without breaking your legs–I think."

"Could you try to be a little more positive?" Rollan asked.

The boy smiled, then jumped into the hole.

Rollan took a deep breath, squeezed his eyes shut, and leaped after the boy.

At first, there was nothing. And then, after an eternity, Rollan slammed into the water below, his breath knocked out of him. He surfaced, then immediately started swimming. A few seconds later, Abeke splashed into the water, followed by Tasha and Dante.

They pulled themselves onto a small sandstone ledge. The boy led them through a series of interconnected caverns. The stone walls varied in color from bloodred to stark white. Stalactites hung above them like chandeliers in a fancy ballroom. Rollan placed his hand on the wall to one of the caves. It was cooler than he expected.

"Many years ago, a tributary of the Nilo River flowed through here," their guide said, pointing to what looked like a dried riverbed. "Now all that remains are these hollowed-out sandstone caves." He eventually stopped upon reaching a long, jagged crack in the rock wall. He pushed through with Rollan close behind. It was another cave almost totally concealed from view.

The boy led them to a large outcropping of boulders at the back of the hidden cave. "I doubt they'll come this far," he said. "But we'd better hide, just to be sure."

They remained quiet for a while, waiting for any guards to show up.

"I think we're safe," the boy said after some time had passed. "Though we may want to stay here until nightfall."

"We'll have to find somewhere else to hide for the night," Abeke said. "Otto is sure to have more guards waiting for us at the harbor."

"I think we have worse problems," Tasha said. "Something's wrong with Dante."

Dante lay slumped over behind a rock. He had already rolled up his sleeve and had tied a cloth around his bicep. There were two small puncture marks below his elbow. Around the bite, his brown skin had turned red and swollen.

"Dante?" Rollan whispered as he inspected his arm. "Why didn't you say anything?"

"I really thought it was just as scratch," he mumbled. "Didn't realize it was swelling until we were running through the alley."

Abeke turned to the boy. "What's your name?" she asked him.

"Madeo," he said.

"Our friend needs help," she said. "Is there someone in town who can attend to his wound?"

Madeo nodded. "There's a woman who lives near the market. Sayyidah Iolya. She will help, but it will come at a price."

Rollan tightened the cloth tie around Dante's arm. "Fine. We'll pay whatever is required. Just take us there." Rollan helped Dante to his feet. "And hurry," he added, as images of Tarik flashed through his mind. "We don't have much time."

THE SULFUR SEA

MEILIN WOKE UP TO FIND HER FACE PRESSED AGAINST black sand. She sat up, brushed the grit from her cheeks, and let her eyes adjust to the endless darkness. Slowly, she made out the lapping sea ahead of them. It seemed to stretch out forever.

Conor was still asleep. Quietly, she pulled back the cloak that he had been using as a cover. The parasite was at the base of his neck. It would make it to his forehead soon. Their only chance to save him was to find and destroy the Wyrm. Which, without Xanthe as their guide, would be much more difficult.

Meilin wished she could go back in time and change how she had treated Xanthe. She knew she had been cruel and cold to the girl, but Meilin didn't like being led around. It wasn't something she was accustomed to. How could she assess the correct path and strategy for her team when she didn't even know which way was north or south? She had lashed out at Xanthe, especially when Xanthe tried to explain how she was navigating the many underground tunnels. It wasn't like Xanthe had memorized a map. She was staking their very lives on her intuition—her hocus-pocus-based navigation.

Meilin looked at the design on the back of her hand. Who was she to question Xanthe's spiritual connection to Sadre? She and Jhi were more than enough evidence that the world above was just as magical. Some things were not meant to be explained. They just were.

Meilin began packing up their meager supplies. She would have traded their entire collection of rockweed for one of Rollan's silly jokes right now. His smiling face was the one she always searched for when things were at their worst. But thanks to Kovo, she was stuck underground while Rollan was up above. She wondered which other Great Beasts had returned. Hopefully, he and Abeke had been more successful than she and Conor.

Takoda joined her at their campsite, dragging the large paddle behind him. "Are you rested enough?" Takoda asked.

"No. Not that it matters." She reached out her hand. "So you finished the paddle?"

Nodding, he hoisted it up and handed it to her. As she took it, Meilin noticed the redness of his palms, the peeling of his skin. She bounced the paddle in her hands, testing its weight. It was still plenty solid, but not too heavy for Kovo, and the rounded handle would be easy for him to grip. Likewise, she figured that the large, flat end of the paddle would be adequate enough to propel them through the water. She would have preferred a sail to navigate the underground winds, but that would have been difficult to make in such limited time, with such threadbare supplies.

"It looks good," she said, handing it back. Then, after a moment, she added, "Thank you."

Takoda looked at the gourd. "I guess we should start packing up the boat."

She heard the sadness in his voice. "Do you want eat first, and then go? We can take a few more minutes—"

"No," he replied. "It would better if we ate while we traveled. No point in wasting any more time."

He walked off toward the boat. Meilin let him go. Takoda was struggling enough with Xanthe's disappearance as it was, and Meilin didn't think she had the words to comfort him.

But she knew who *did*.

She touched the tattoo on the back of her hand, and Jhi appeared in the sand beside her. "I'm going to wake Conor," she told the panda. "Is there anything you can do to help Takoda?"

After Jhi left, Meilin knelt beside Conor and touched his arm. Slowly, his eyes batted open. "Huh . . . Meilin?" He sat up and yawned. "How long was I asleep?"

"Not very long," Meilin said. She didn't know exactly how long he had been asleep—this eternal darkness made tracking time nearly impossible—but she knew he'd slept longer than usual. "Are you ready?" she asked him.

He nodded as he scratched behind Briggan's ears. "Do you think I'll have to put Briggan in his dormant state?"

Meilin looked at the sea. It seemed fairly smooth for now, but she had no idea what awaited them farther in. "I'll leave that to you and Briggan to decide," she said.

"There should be enough room in the boat for him, if that's what you want."

"I just . . . I don't know if I can trust myself. Especially if I have to lead us to the Wyrm. I don't know what that will do to the parasite." He shrugged. "And don't try to argue with me. It's our best plan."

Meilin remained still. Conor had first mentioned that he could sense the Wyrm when they were cleaning the gourd. She hadn't wanted to use his connection to lead them to it, but without Xanthe, she didn't see any other option. "That's a lot to ask of you," she finally said, her words measured.

"But you would do the same," he said, cutting into her with his clear blue eyes. He had changed so much, from the ruddy-faced shepherd from Eura to one of the Heroes of Erdas. He was slimmer. Taller. Less naive and more ingrained in this new life of battles, danger, and quests.

She desperately missed the old Conor.

"You will be okay," she said. "I believe in you. Remember how I fought Gerathon's Bile? You can do the same. Use the Wyrm, but don't let it control you."

"Okay," Conor said. "But I need you to promise me something."

Meilin already knew where this was going. "No, Conor."

He moved so he was sitting right in front of her. "If the time comes . . . *when* the times comes that the parasite takes over my body, you have to stop me. I can't become one of them. One of the Many."

Meilin glanced at her hands. She didn't want to picture using them to fight Conor. But she also didn't want to see him turn into one of the Wyrm's mindless minions. "We'll . . . figure something out," Meilin stammered. "We'll bring ropes. We . . . we can tie you up."

"And if that doesn't work?"

Meilin finally looked back up and slowly nodded. "Then I'll stop you," she promised. "One way or another."

She rose then, and joined Takoda and Jhi at the boat. Takoda seemed much more relaxed than before. Meilin knew that Jhi must have used her powers to soothe him. Meilin herself wouldn't have made it through some of her darker days without the Great Beast.

As Jhi walked toward Meilin, she kept stopping to shake excess sand from her black-and-white fur. After a few feeble attempts, Jhi plopped down on her rear and waited for Meilin to come to her.

"Lazy panda," Meilin said with a grin. "I know you don't like the beach, but be careful what you wish for." She rubbed the panda's paws, trying to brush off as much sand as she could, then pulled her to passive state. She would keep Jhi away for as long as possible, but she'd eventually have to come out to care for Conor.

Takoda and Meilin didn't speak as they began loading their equipment into the gourd. Conor joined them a few moments later, lugging some of the supplies from their campsite. Kovo sat a few feet away, his arms defiantly crossed, but Meilin didn't want to ask him for help. The ape would be doing most of the rowing anyway.

She picked up her quarterstaff and placed it in the boat. It felt funny in her hands—it was too short and didn't have the proper weight—but she refused to leave it behind. It was one of the few weapons that remained. They had lost almost everything when fleeing Phos Astos, and the rest while sprinting across the burning Arachane Fields.

Once all the supplies were loaded, Takoda called for Kovo. The Great Beast huffed and grunted, but helped them to push the boat into the water.

"Is he upset about rowing?" Conor asked once the boat bobbed in the sea.

"No," Takoda replied. "He just doesn't like the water." Then he nodded at Briggan, who was timidly pawing at the wet beach. "Perhaps he'd be more comfortable in passive state?"

"Conor and Briggan are fine," Meilin snapped. She immediately regretted her tone, but at the same time, she didn't want Takoda to make Conor feel self-conscious, even unintentionally. Water splashed onto her boots and legs as she made her way to the boat. She climbed in. "Let's go."

Conor and Briggan followed, then Takoda. Finally, Kovo climbed into the boat. The gourd sank with the addition of each passenger, but remained above water. Kovo positioned himself at the rear of the boat. He jammed the end of the paddle through the shallow water to the sandy bottom of the sea and pushed them away from the beach.

"So what's the plan?" Takoda asked. "There's a small current. We can let that carry us for a while. That way, Kovo won't tire himself out."

"Well, let's see if that's even the correct way," Meilin asked. "Conor?"

The boy looked paler than usual as he nodded. With one hand on Briggan, he closed his eyes. His breath started slowly at first, then increased at an alarming rate. Sweat poured down his face, and his body began to shake. The parasite at the base of his neck seemed to tremble as well. Meilin wasn't sure, but it almost looked as if the black mark was moving. . . .

"Conor, snap out of it!" she yelled as the parasite pulsed and wriggled a little higher. She couldn't let him do this. "Conor!"

"To the left!" he shouted, his eyes flashing open. He pointed a shaky hand toward an invisible point on the water's horizon. "There. That's where we want to go."

Meilin positioned herself beside Conor. "Are you okay?" After he nodded, she asked, "What did you see?"

"Not see," he finally said. "Feel." He wiped the sweat from his forehead. "I felt evil."

Meilin had no idea how long it would take to reach the base of the Evertree. They had been in the boat for hours and didn't seem any closer to finding it than when they departed. For the most part, they traveled with the current, though Kovo still had to use the paddle when the current shifted and pulled them in different directions.

She had finally ordered everyone to rest. Conor didn't waste any time, falling asleep as soon as he lay down. Takoda was more reluctant, but eventually he closed his eyes. Just before falling asleep, he suggested that she rest as well—that Kovo could take the first watch.

No way, Meilin thought. For all she knew, Kovo would capsize the boat and try to drown them all before continuing on to defeat—or maybe even partner with—the Wyrm himself. Or perhaps he would cast Conor overboard. Kovo hadn't bothered to hide his feelings about the boy. As soon as Conor fell asleep, Kovo and Takoda began signing passionately, with the ape repeatedly flipping his hands over, and then pointing to Conor. Each time, Takoda would pinch two fingers and his thumb together, shake his head, and reply with a resounding *No*.

Things looked bleak, but as long as Conor was fighting the effects of the parasite, she wouldn't abandon him.

But what would happen if he finally succumbed?

Meilin knew what it was like to not be in control of her own actions, to fight against another will for control of her body. During her Nectar Ceremony—when she summoned Jhi as her spirit animal—her father had secretly given her a concoction called the Bile. It was supposed to ensure that she would summon an animal. Instead, it made her a slave to Gerathon the Serpent, forcing her to do the evil Great Beast's bidding.

Even now, Meilin still remembered the look on Abeke's and Rollan's faces as Gerathon forced her to attack them. Meilin could hear the sound of her staff crashing down on Abeke's head, right before she captured her and delivered her to the Conquerors like a good little mindless soldier.

Meilin had been lucky—she had been able to avoid seriously hurting her friends, and thanks to Tellun, she had finally become free of the Bile. But could Conor hope for the same? And if Conor really *did* attack her or Takoda, would she be willing to do what was necessary to stop him?

She wondered if she should release Jhi. She could use the panda's comfort, and Conor could use her healing abilities. *I'll release her once Conor wakes*, she told herself. *I will not lose him without a fight.*

Meilin pulled her cloak around her arms and repositioned herself in the boat. Across from her, Kovo looked out at the sea. She followed his gaze.

Perhaps he saw something beyond the choppy yellow waves. Meilin searched as well. The water seemed to be breaking against something. Land? A reef? Or a ship? Yes, a ship! The *Tellun's Pride* cut through the mustard-colored water. Rollan stood on the bow of the ship, his worn green cloak rustling in the breeze. He was smiling and waving, and then he was frowning and shouting, although he was too far away for Meilin to hear him. She leaned closer, and closer, and—

She jerked up. There was no ship, and no Rollan. She had fallen asleep! Across from her, Kovo stared at her, smiling. *Weakling*, his eyes seemed to be saying.

Meilin sat up, forcing herself into a less comfortable position.

More hours passed. Meilin felt herself drifting off a few times, but was always able to snap awake before she fully embraced sleep. She glanced at Kovo. He sat perfectly still, with the large paddle in his lap. His eyes were closed, and his nostrils slowly brought air in and pushed it out. The mighty Kovo had fallen asleep. *Ha!* Who was the weakling now?

She was just about to wake up the others when she saw a luminous orb glowing in the distance. It almost looked like a smaller version of the sun, or perhaps a full moon, but they were underground. That was impossible. She pinched herself, just to make sure that she wasn't asleep.

As they approached the orb, Meilin realized that it seemed to be hovering in the air. She thought about the glowing spheres that Takoda had found. They weren't nearly as bright as this one. If she could grab it, they wouldn't have to sit in this eternal darkness.

Meilin stood up slowly, so that she wouldn't rock the boat. The orb was almost within reach. She raised herself on her tiptoes, stretched her arms out, and grabbed it with both hands. It was warm and sticky, but at least the tacky gunk covering it made it easier to hold.

But it wasn't until she grabbed it that she realized the orb wasn't actually floating. It was hanging from something. She could now clearly see what looked like a dark gray, sinewy tree branch attached to it. The branch arched high, then disappeared into the water. What type of tree was this?

She tugged hard on the orb, hoping that she could pull it from the branch. Suddenly, the water around them churned, and the orb began to pull away. Meilin tried to drop it, but it was stuck to her! The tacky substance on the orb's surface had glued her hands to it.

The vine jerked violently away from the boat. Meilin stumbled forward. Her foot caught on the edge of the gourd, and she felt herself falling overboard. She squeezed her eyes shut and braced herself for the impact against the water—but something large and meaty grabbed her waist, stopping her from falling over.

Kovo!

He snarled at her as he pulled her back into the boat. Immediately, the orb began jerking away again, causing Meilin's arms to yank forward. Kovo grabbed the branch, or whatever it was, and tore it away from the orb.

With the tension from the branch immediately released, Meilin fell backward onto her rear, the orb still in her hands. Takoda was awake by now, and Conor was trying to untangle himself from his cloak.

"What's going on?" Takoda yelled.

"I don't know," Meilin said, scrambling back to her feet. "I saw this orb and I grabbed it, thinking we could use the light. But now it's stuck to my hands."

Conor pointed toward the water. "What's that?"

Something was moving underwater. It crested, and everyone gasped. It looked like a deformed, mutated version of an anglerfish. Meilin had heard of them—deep-sea hunters who lured their prey with brightly lit antennas. Double rows of jagged teeth lined the top and bottom of the fish's gaping mouth. Its translucent skin was covered in long spikes. It seemed to look right at Meilin with its large black eyes as it sped toward the boat.

"It's going to ram us!" Meilin yelled. "Hold on."

The fish exploded into the side of the boat, causing it to teeter dangerously to the left. Briggan howled as he slid toward the edge. Conor leaped forward and grabbed the wolf before he fell into the water.

"It's circling back around!" Takoda said.

Kovo rushed to the side of the boat and stared as the fish raced toward them. He raised the paddle high above his head and brought it down right as the fish rammed into the boat again. The boat tilted sharply once more, and Takoda and Kovo went flying. Meilin jumped in the opposite direction, ramming her shoulder against the inside of the gourd in an attempt to stop it from turning completely over.

"Get to the center!" Meilin shouted. "Otherwise, we'll sink!"

Everyone crawled to the middle of the boat and waited. At first it continued to rock violently, but after a few tense moments it slowed to a slight bob.

"Is it gone?" Conor asked.

"Yes, I think so," Takoda replied. "Kovo must have stopped it." He turned to his spirit animal and made a sign with his hands. Meilin had been seeing him use it more and more lately. *Thank you.*

Instead of replying, the Great Beast moved to the edge of the boat and looked into the water.

Takoda frowned. "Kovo? What is wrong? Do you think the fish is going to attack again?"

Kovo shook his head. He made a rowing motion with his hands, then pointed behind him.

"What?" Meilin asked. "You want to go in a different direction?" She turned to Conor. "Is that the way to the Wyrm?"

"It's the paddle," Takoda said. "Kovo must have dropped it during the last attack. It's out there, somewhere in the sea."

Meilin began frantically searching the water. "Does anyone see it?" She held up the orb, which was still stuck to her hands. "It's probably somewhere behind us."

"Even if it *is* back there, how are we going to reach it?" Takoda asked. "We don't have any way to paddle backward. And we can't swim with creatures like that in the water."

"So we're just supposed to sit here, do nothing, and let the current take us who knows where?" Meilin asked.

"It could be worse. At least we have a current," Takoda said. "We should take inventory. I saw at least one bundle of supplies fly overboard."

Conor knelt in front of Meilin and inspected her hands. "Here, let me help you with that." They both pulled, and eventually Conor was able to pry the orb from her palms, but not without taking a few layers of skin in the process.

Meilin wanted to kick the stupid orb into the water. They were adrift, without a way to navigate, and their handful of limited supplies had just become smaller.

They were at the total mercy of the Sulfur Sea, and it was all Meilin's fault.

SAYYIDAH IOLYA

TASHA SAT IN THE CORNER OF THE SMALL, SIMPLE, one-room hut with Rollan, Abeke, and Madeo, and took in another spoonful of vegetable soup. Well, she wasn't actually sure *what* was in the soup, but thinking that the gray blobs floating in the brown liquid were some type of exotic root calmed her stomach. Abeke had almost finished her bowl, while Rollan and Madeo had already moved on to seconds. She would have given anything for some of Dante's special spices right then.

Across the room, Sayyidah Iolya, an elderly, hunch-backed woman, tended to Dante. He had barely been able to stand when they reached the woman's home. Once they described what had happened to him—and paid—she began preparing a solution for his arm in a large copper pot. Whatever the elixir was, it smelled even worse than the vegetable soup. Dante had screamed in pain when she first poured it over his swollen fore-arm. Now he was silent, and Tasha had no idea if this was better or worse.

After wrapping Dante's arm in a bandage, Sayyidah Iolya hobbled to them. "Your father was struck by a red-striped cottonmouth," she said to Rollan. "He's lucky that the bite was shallow . . . and that you reached me when you did. If the snake had sunk its fangs farther into his flesh, he would already be dead and rotting."

"Thank you," Rollan said. "And he's *not* my father."

Tasha caught the edge in Rollan's voice. She thought about their conversation in Stetriol, about the Greencloak who had been like a father to him. She knew he was no longer alive, though Rollan hadn't told her what had happened to him.

Sayyidah Iolya tapped her knotted, wooden cane on the dirt floor. "Whoever he is, he must remain here for four days. It will take that long for the poison and my antidote to work their way through his system." The woman grinned a crooked, toothless smile. "You realize that the lodging will cost extra, yes?"

Rollan scowled as he pulled a few coins from his bag. "Just in case you didn't recognize the cloaks, we're the good guys."

The woman took the coins and inspected them against a nearby candle flame. "Greencloak, Conqueror, merchant—I don't care what colors or emblems you wear, as long as you carry gold."

Tasha waited for the woman to return to Dante. "At least she didn't charge us for the vegetable soup," she said.

Rollan slowly turned to her. "Tasha, those aren't vegetables."

Tasha's stomach gurgled. "Do I want to know—?"

"No," Abeke, Rollan, and Madeo said at the same time.

Tasha put her bowl down on the gritty floor. Even at its worst, her life in Stetriol was nothing like this. "So now what do we do?"

"We can't wait for Dante to heal," Abeke said. "Madeo, do you know of any secret entrances into Zourtzi?"

Madeo's eyes widened. "The island fortress is impenetrable, and its sentries are cruel. None of us would dare try to sneak in," he said. "Which is too bad. Faisel's always throwing feasts. Some of the kids heard that he feeds entire cases of leftover hens to his hunting hounds."

"We have word that he's preparing another feast for his son to celebrate the arrival of Cabaro," Abeke said.

Madeo nodded. "A seven-day festival. Ships are set to arrive tomorrow. My friends at the pier say that they're coming from as far as Amaya."

Rollan and Abeke shared a long glance. "Word is spreading," Abeke said. "For all we know, Zerif may be on his way."

"With an army of infected Greencloaks at his side," Rollan muttered. "As if this day couldn't get any worse."

"There may be a way inside," Madeo said. "For festivals this large, Sealy, the head chef, has brought in children to work as servants. He never picks the street kids, instead getting children from 'respectable' families who live by the river. Sealy's already chosen his servants, but I'll bet I can find three who are willing to swap places with you . . . for the right price."

Abeke nodded. "I suppose that'll have to work."

"I'll send word tonight, and will meet you back here at dawn with your servants' clothes." Madeo rose from the floor and looked at Abeke. "Many of my friends love Cabaro, because he's a lion and from Nilo. But I was always the fastest of my family. My favorite is Uraza."

Abeke smiled, and in a flash, Uraza appeared. The leopard cautiously approached Madeo.

"You can touch her," Abeke said. "She's kind to those who are kind to her."

The boy slowly placed his hand on the large beast's back. "While Faisel and his family remained safe in Zourtzi, the rest of Caylif fell to the Conquerors," Madeo said. "It was hard for us to survive. Many didn't." He removed his hand and took a step back. "Thank you for saving us."

And with that, the boy exited the hut.

Tasha released Ninani. The bird sniffed at her bowl but didn't eat. "Is being a Greencloak always like this?" she asked. "People expect so much of you. When I was home, all I had to worry about were completing my studies and tending to my chores."

"Such is the life of a Greencloak," Abeke said. "Though having a Great Beast draws even more attention." Abeke petted Uraza, and she murmured a deep purr in response. "But as you just saw, it can also be rewarding."

"We want you with us, on our side," Rollan said. "But you don't have to decide today. You have time."

"But if Greenhaven has fallen, are there any Greencloaks left?" Tasha asked. "Is there even anything remaining to join?"

"There will always be Greencloaks," Abeke said. She

stretched out and pulled her cloak around herself, almost like a sleeping bag. "We'd better get some rest. Tomorrow will be a long day."

"But at least we won't have to eat rat stew if we're working as servants," Rollan added.

Tasha's stomach churned. "Rats? You're joking, right?"

Rollan's laughter was the only response she received.

7

ZOURTZI

ABEKE TRIED NOT TO TUG AT HER STIFF GRAY SHIRT AND long, itchy black skirt. Madeo had been able to find three kids willing to give up their posts for a little free coin, while Abeke, Rollan, and Tasha took their places as servants. Abeke's skirt had been too long, but Tasha was able to quickly alter the hem to shorten it.

Abeke and Tasha stood at the edge of the pier along with twenty other girls. Rollan stood in a parallel line with the boys.

Two piers away, a group of uniformed guards stood in front of the *Tellun's Pride II*.

A pair of large guards, both dressed in black tunics and boots, stood at the front of each line. As the children stepped forward one by one, the guards gave them a quick once-over, then made a small mark on a parchment before allowing them to proceed onto the sailboat. Madeo and the other children had told Abeke not to worry about the list. The men checking them in had no idea what their servants looked like—they only had their names. Abeke had easily memorized her new name. She hoped Tasha had done the same.

Tasha was fidgeting in front of her, continually loosening and rebraiding a strand of her white-blond hair. Abeke placed her hand on the girl's shoulder. "Try to remain calm," she whispered. "Act like you belong."

Abeke picked up her backpack and took another step forward. She had been able to stuff her and Tasha's cloaks inside the bag, but she'd had to leave her bow and arrows with Sayyidah Iolya. Madeo had promised to check in on Dante and fill him in on the plan. When Rollan tried to give Madeo the rest of the money, he had declined, saying he couldn't take any more money from the Heroes of Erdas.

There were only two children in front of them when Abeke heard a familiar voice.

"Sealy! I know you're in there!"

She glanced behind her. Otto, the merchant from the silk shop, limped past them, a new shiny black obsidian cane clacking with every other step. The guard at the front of the pier didn't speak, instead jerking his head to the boat. Otto grumbled but clumsily climbed the ramp and stepped onto the deck. He disappeared into a small cabin.

Tasha turned around. "Abeke—"

"Lower your voice," Abeke whispered. They took a step forward as another girl was allowed onto the boat. "Don't worry. Nothing will happen if you don't draw attention to yourself."

"We destroyed his shop yesterday," Tasha countered. "Dante sliced his leg. He's going to recognize us."

Abeke knew that they had to get inside Zourtzi, and that this was their only chance. But she also didn't want her desperation to cloud her judgment. She looked over and caught Rollan's eye. She raised an eyebrow as a question. He shook his head in response.

They were in agreement. They were getting on that boat.

"Just keep moving," she whispered, giving Tasha a slight nudge.

As Tasha reached the front of the line, Otto emerged from the cabin. Tasha was checked in and moved toward the boat as Otto began to hobble down the ramp.

Abeke placed her hand on her sleeve and readied herself to call Uraza. But as Tasha boarded, Otto walked right past her, not even glancing in her direction.

Abeke lowered her hand, told the steward her name, and stepped onto the boat. Rollan joined her and Tasha a few moments later.

"How did you know he wouldn't notice us?" Tasha asked. "I walked right by him. He had to have seen me."

"He's a rich, important man," Abeke replied. "And we are servants."

"It would be beneath him to even look at us," Rollan added. "To him, kids like us barely exist."

Tasha chewed on her lip as she looked out onto the harbor. Abeke didn't know much about Tasha's background, other than that she was probably wealthier than Abeke and Rollan. Unlike either of them, Tasha still had both of her parents.

Abeke wondered what her own mother would have said if she had been alive during Abeke's Nectar

Ceremony. If she had seen Abeke call Uraza. From what she remembered of her, Abeke knew her mother would have reacted much more positively than her father had.

After all the children boarded, the sailboat departed.

"At least the *Tellun's Pride II* is still there," Rollan whispered as they passed the ship. "Though with the number of men guarding it, I don't see us boarding anytime soon."

"We'll have to worry about that later," Abeke said. "I'm sure Dante could help us find another way out of Nilo." She smiled. "Or maybe we could hide in my village. Soama could certainly make a meal better than rat stew."

Tasha groaned. "Seriously. Was that really rat stew that I had been eating?" She covered her mouth. "I think I should sit down. I'm going to be seasick."

Abeke, Rollan, and Tasha found a quiet spot along the railing to sit. Some of the other kids talked and joked with each other, but Abeke felt it was best if they kept to themselves. She still wasn't convinced that Tasha would be able to speak to the other children without revealing who they really were.

The sailboat, aided by the current and a fast wind, easily outpaced the larger, heavier boats in the open sea. It wasn't long until the majestic fort loomed before them. It was even more spectacular up close. The walls were white and almost looked polished. And its four towers seemed to stretch to the sun.

Rollan pointed to the water. "What types of rocks are those?"

Abeke frowned at the row of pale, angular shapes just underneath the water's surface. The boat cruised a few lengths away from them. Any closer and the rocks would have cut deep gashes into the ship's hull.

"It's some type of cement," Tasha said. "It's man-made."

"So they somehow created a rock reef to ward off ships?" Rollan asked. "Hopefully it's easier to get out of this place than in."

The boat slowed as it neared the stone-bricked pier. The children lined up and disembarked onto a wide gangplank once it had docked. The pier connected to a large promenade shaded by billowing palm and juniper trees. Up ahead, a large, manicured lawn stretched out before a series of wide, steep ivory steps. The steps were like a triangle, wide at the bottom and slowly narrowing as they reached the massive granite double doors at their apex.

Abeke tried not to stare at the guards lined along the steps. Unlike the typical Niloan garb, they all wore black clothes with heavy metal chain mail. Some wore stripes on their shoulders. *Perhaps it's some type of rank*, she thought. Each carried a long, curved sword, similar to the ones that the men at the silk shop had used.

She and the others were ushered through a large foyer and down a massive corridor to the servants' chambers. There, they were greeted by the main servants. Unlike the children's clothes, the regular servant uniform looked much more comfortable and practical.

Abeke was given her initial duties and was then assigned to her sleeping quarters. She, Tasha, and a young, waifish girl with short brown hair were assigned into a room together. However, before the main servants led them to their quarters, Rollan pulled the brown-haired girl to the side and whispered something to her, quietly slipping her a coin. He grinned as he returned to Abeke and Tasha.

"If seems that everyone's a businessperson in this city," he said, picking up Abeke's bag. "Let's go check out our quarters."

The room was small but adequate. Two beds lined the wall farthest from the door, and the other bed stood underneath a small window.

Rollan glanced out the window. "Lucky Essix. Better to be out there than in here." He flopped on the bed, then winced.

Abeke sat down on the hard bed. "Rollan, were you assigned a task?"

He shook his head as he leaned back, placing his hands behind his neck. "I'm supposed to report to the kitchen in an hour for mine," he said.

"Me too," Tasha said. "Since we don't have to report for a while, maybe we should look for Cabaro now."

"I don't think that's wise," Abeke said. "It would arouse too much suspicion if we were seen sneaking around, and it could jeopardize our mission." She opened her bag and pulled out a dagger. "Plus, I already know where to find Cabaro."

Rollan sat up. "What? You sense him with those cat-reflexes of yours?"

"Funny," she said, smiling. "But no, that isn't it. I've been assigned to act as one of Kirat's servants."

"*What?* They're letting us *kids* serve Faisel's family?" Rollan asked. "That doesn't make any sense."

Abeke shrugged. "From the way I understand it, the regular servants are responsible for attending to all the fancy guests arriving later today. We've been relegated to serving the less important people—like his child." She tucked the dagger into her boot and smoothed her dress. "Wish me luck."

Abeke and five other servants stood in the service corridor leading to one of the fortress's many dining chambers. Each servant carried a dish, some two. Abeke held a steaming bowl of warm towels in her hands. Even with the three thick kitchen towels blocking her fingers from the bowl, her skin burned. But she didn't dare complain. Sealy, the head chef, had already reassigned one child when he accidentally spilled a drop of mango juice on the pristine tiled kitchen floor.

"Line up against the far wall as soon as you enter Master Kirat's dining quarters," Ahmar said. He was one of the regular servants and had been tasked with overseeing Abeke's group. "Whatever you do, do not look directly into Kirat's or Cabaro's eyes." He lowered his voice. "Especially Cabaro. He's already maimed two servants. But if you keep your head down and limit any sudden movements, you should come out of this with all your digits intact."

Ahmar knocked on the door three times. When no one answered, he opened the door and led the servants in. The room was massive. Large, scarlet silk curtains hung over each window, casting the room in a dull, reddish tint. Mounted animal heads sat on each wall. Abeke was glad that none of them were leopards.

The focal point of the room was a large, exquisitely carved round wooden table. It was large enough to seat at least twelve people, though only one throne-sized chair stood at the far end. Ahmar placed two gold and ivory utensils on the table, then returned to the wall with the other servants.

The main door swung open. A few men walked in, their boots loud against the floor. They were followed by a tall boy wearing beige linen clothes and gold rings on his fingers. He must have been Kirat.

Then Cabaro appeared.

The girl next to Abeke sucked in her breath, and the plate of eggs wobbled in her hand. Glancing down the line, Abeke could tell that the other servants were equally as rattled.

Cabaro slowly approached the table, his tail lazily swishing back and forth. He looked slightly larger than a normal lion. Like the other reborn Great Beasts, he was a shadow of his former self, yet Abeke reminded herself that he was still a lion.

He yawned, showing all of his white, sharp teeth.

The last time Abeke had seen Cabaro, he had been charging into the Evertree, sacrificing his life to save Erdas. She wondered if any memory of that act remained.

Ahmar snapped to attention as another man entered the room. With the way everyone nodded and bowed at him, including Kirat, he must have been Faisel. His physical traits reminded Abeke of the people of both Zhong and Northern Nilo. She assumed that he was of dual heritage, like Takoda.

Faisel rubbed his graying beard as he inspected the line of servants against the wall. "Do not worry; Cabaro has already eaten." He smiled at the smallest of them—a light-skinned Euran boy with freckles and brown hair. "Though perhaps he would be interested in dessert."

Faisel laughed, filling the silent room. Cabaro yawned again, then flopped down on the floor and began grooming himself. He didn't seem to notice anyone in the room—the servants, the men, or even his human partner, Kirat. The boy had stretched out his arm and was whispering something to the lion, but Cabaro just continued to lick his paws with his tongue.

Faisel turned and saw his son kneeling before the lion. "Kirat," he snapped. The boy jumped to his feet. "Must you display your shortcomings in front of the entire staff?"

"But I thought . . . it felt like—"

"I do not care about your excuses," Faisel said. "Only results." Then he joined the other men. They had pulled off to a corner of the room. "When will my son learn how to force his animal into a dormant state?" he demanded, his voice overshadowing all others. "I am paying you far too much for these continued failures."

Abeke felt sorry for Kirat as the men tried to explain what she already knew. It required trust for a spirit animal to willingly enter the dormant state. It had taken almost a week for Uraza to trust her enough to become passive, and even longer for Rollan and the independent Essix. There was no telling how long it would take Cabaro—if ever. But from her limited observations of Faisel, she could tell that anything other than immediate success would be considered a disappointment.

Kirat slipped into the large chair. "I'm ready to begin," he said, his voice stronger than before.

Ahmar walked to the table, unrolled a linen napkin, and draped it across Kirat's lap. Then he clapped his hands. The first two servants moved forward. One placed a glass of juice in front of the boy, and the other placed a plate of fruit.

Kirat took three bites of his fruit and a sip of the juice. "Next," he commanded.

Abeke frowned as Ahmar collected the plates. *He's finished already?*

This continued with each plate. Eggs, smoked fish, baked bread—no matter the food, Kirat only took a few bites before discarding the plate. How could he be so wasteful, when an entire city was starving just beyond his walls?

"Towels," he snapped.

It took Ahmar clearing his throat for Abeke to realize that this was her cue. She quickly crossed the room and placed the warm bowl before Kirat. Like Otto the merchant and all the other important people she had encountered, Kirat refused to meet her gaze.

Suddenly, one of the servants shrieked.

Abeke turned around. Cabaro had risen to his feet and was walking toward her!

Kirat stood as well. "Cabaro! Be still!"

The lion almost seemed to laugh at the boy's command—a low, rumbling sound issued from his throat. He continued forward, his tail now dragging against the floor. Perhaps Kirat would not look at Abeke, but Cabaro did. He gazed at her almost quizzically. It was as if he recognized her, but he didn't know how, or from where.

Abeke placed her hand on her sleeve but didn't move. She didn't want to call Uraza, but if he attacked, she wouldn't have any choice.

"Ahmar, summon the guards," Kirat said.

"You will do no such thing," Faisel said, crossing the room. "I will not have one hair on this magnificent beast harmed."

Cabaro took another step toward Abeke and sniffed the air. His eyes flashed. It seemed he suddenly realized who she was—and also probably realized which Great Beast she could call forth. Abeke had grown up hearing stories of the rivalry between Uraza and Cabaro. Both were native to Nilo. Both claimed to be the greatest hunter in the land.

Cabaro continued to glare at Abeke. He bared his teeth but didn't roar or advance. She wasn't sure, but it almost seemed as if his gaze kept shifting from Abeke's eyes to her arm. Then he snorted and withdrew, his eyes on Abeke the entire time. He flopped back onto the floor and returned to grooming himself.

Abeke slowly lowered her hand. Was Cabaro afraid to face Uraza? Or was he merely too lazy to be bothered with a confrontation right then?

Faisel clapped his hands and laughed, breaking the tension in the room. "It seems that Cabaro has finally met his match." He pointed to Abeke but kept his eyes on his son. "For the rest of the week, she will act as your primary server. And if you're lucky, maybe she'll also teach you how to control your lion."

FAST FRIENDS

ROLLAN BROKE OFF A SMALL PIECE OF THE LOAF OF bread that Sayyidah Iolya had given them and tossed it to Essix. Essix stared at the bread for a few seconds, then pushed it around with her beak.

"Trust me," he said, popping a piece into his mouth. "It's actually pretty good."

Essix finally picked up the bread, tilted her head back, and swallowed it whole.

Rollan was surprised that Essix had remained in the small room for as long as she had. She hated enclosed spaces. But having her here was good. Focusing on Essix took his mind off other things. Other people. Abeke. Dante. Conor.

Meilin.

He squeezed the stiff loaf of bread. Here he was, safely hidden away in one of the most spectacular fortresses he had ever seen, while Meilin was trapped underground with Takoda and Conor . . . and Kovo, easily the most menacing and untrustworthy of the Great

Beasts. She would have loved Zourtzi—the architecture was a mix of Niloan and Zhongese styles. Perhaps it would have reminded her of home.

And what about Conor? Even with the healing properties of Jhi, how much longer could Conor last before the parasite took total control of his body and mind? Rollan had seen firsthand what the parasite could do. He was sure that he'd never forget the empty look in Arac's eyes as Rollan fought him on the deck of the *Tellun's Pride II*. He'd never forget the way Arac's body twisted and turned as it fell overboard into the dark sea. Rollan had only known Arac for a few days and was still haunted by his attack. How would Meilin feel if Conor attacked *her*?

Essix flapped her wings, getting Rollan's attention. "Okay, but after this, I'm cutting you off," he said, tossing her another piece of bread. Then he glanced at Tasha. "Why don't you find some *rats* to chew on or something?"

Tasha groaned on the other side of the room. "Not funny!" Like Rollan, she was feeding her spirit animal. She tossed a piece of bread to Ninani, but it went way off the mark and instead hit the wall behind the swan.

"I thought Ninani was supposed to make you more graceful."

She sighed. "That *is* more graceful."

Rollan laughed. "So what was life like for you before we showed up? I'm guessing that they didn't serve a lot of rodent delicacies in that fancy castle you were living in."

Now Tasha laughed. "I was practically a stranger in

that castle. I had only been living there for a few days before you and Abeke arrived. Even then, I wasn't permitted to roam the halls by myself. There was always some official looking over me, taking notes and scribbling down everything that Ninani and I did." Ninani waddled to her, and she began to stroke the white swan's back. "Before the war, my family lived in a small village farther inland, close to the mountains. My father was the town's farrier." Rollan must have been frowning, because she said, "A farrier is kind of like a blacksmith, but only for horses. The terrain in Stetriol is very rocky. When it comes to hauling equipment or plowing fields, a horse without a good pair of shoes is about as useful as a potbellied pig."

"I'd take a pig over a horse any day," Rollan murmured. "So what happened when the war broke out? Did your father become one of the Conquerors?"

"They asked him, but he refused. He saw what that drink did to the animals—"

"Bile," Rollan said. He could hear the contempt in his voice.

"Yes, the Bile. They had used it on some horses in his care. Most bulked up immediately, transforming from quiet, graceful creatures into something twisted and sinister. I thought that was bad, until I saw what happened when an animal couldn't take the transition. The horses would shudder and break down and . . ." Her voice trailed off as she shook her head. "So no, my father refused to drink the Bile and join the Reptile King's army. They instead used him as a blacksmith. But not for the animals. He made weapons. Swords, axes, whatever they required." She fed Ninani the last of her bread. "He hated it, but it allowed him to provide for us. Food was always scarce, but we never went hungry." Tasha looked at Rollan, and her blue eyes cut into him. "What was life like for you before the war?"

"Less fighting. More rats." He stood up. "Sometimes, I think I preferred the rats."

"But you chose this path. You chose to be a Greencloak. Why?"

"We all have a duty. Even a street kid like me." Rollan scooped up Essix and walked to the window. "See you tonight," he said to the falcon. "Do me a favor and check on Dante, okay? And let me know if you see any messages from Lenori or Olvan."

The bird seemed to nod in acknowledgment, then took off.

Rollan thought about trying to tap into Essix's vision, but decided against it. He didn't want to become sick again, not when he'd have to report to the kitchen soon. Still, he wanted to get a better look at Zourtzi. If it was really that impenetrable, then maybe Zerif wouldn't be able to enter after all. Maybe Cabaro would be better off staying here. And perhaps it would be safe for other spirit animals as well. Tasha wanted to be a Greencloak, but she needed time to think about what she was signing up for. She needed a safe place to think. And maybe this was it.

He turned to see that Tasha had risen from the floor. The sunlight shining in through the window caught her braided hair. It was piled high on her head, and the sunlight made it look that much blonder. "What are you thinking about?" she asked.

"Just wondering if they're going to make me serve the

fortress's dogs or Faisel himself," he said. "Not that one's better than the other."

Tasha continued toward him. She rose up on her toes and peered out the window. "Abeke warned me that you were good at evading people," she said. "She was right."

He rubbed the back of his head. "It takes me a while to warm up to people. Back home, you couldn't really trust anyone, not even other orphans. They'd get close to you, only to steal your clothes or food. Or turn you in to the militia. Or worst, the orphanages."

"But you came to trust the Greencloaks," she said. "Was it because of the man you mentioned before? Travis?"

"Tarik," Rollan corrected. Just saying his name out loud made Rollan's throat hurt. "Yes, he was a great mentor, and someone I came to trust with my life. But he wasn't the only reason I joined. Abeke, Conor, and Meilin had a lot to do with it as well." He frowned as a large smile spread across Tasha's face. "What?" he demanded.

"Nothing. Just the way your face looked when you mentioned Meilin's name," she said. "It's clear that you care about her."

"You would like her. Eventually," he said. "You'd especially like Conor. He's a lot like you, but less clumsy. And he's one of the kindest, most loyal people I've ever met."

Tasha's face fell. "There it was again. Something in your face—in your voice—when you talked about Conor. Is he okay?"

Rollan squinted at Ninani. "Are you doing this to her?" he asked. "Enhancing her senses or something? Or is she always this inquisitive?"

Ninani flapped her wings. He wasn't exactly sure, but he thought that the swan might have winked at him.

"All right, enough with all the talking." He pulled a dagger from his bag and, like Abeke, slid it inside his boot. "Time to go to work."

9

LAREIMAJA

WITH AS MUCH FOOD AS WAS STACKED ON TOP OF THE kitchen counters, it was apparent that Sealy and his staff had been cooking since early that morning. However, there wasn't a drop of food on his immaculate white linen jacket.

He frowned at each of the children lined up against the wall. "Let me be clear," he said. "You all are the worst of the worst. The only reason you all even made it inside the fortress is because I needed forty servants instead of twenty-five." He stopped in front of a small boy. Tasha assumed that he couldn't be much older than eight. He was supposed to be outside, playing with his friends, not getting yelled at by an oversized bully.

"Most of you will be responsible for cleaning the floors and the horse stalls. Some get to polish those ivory stairs outside. But two of you get the *extreme* honor of tending to Lady LaReimaja." He continued walking. "So who will it be?"

None of the kids moved forward. It really said something about the family's reputation that the kids would pick mopping and sweeping to serving Faisel's wife. Tasha looked at Rollan, hoping to catch his attention, but his eyes remained glued to the ground.

There was a quiet cough to Tasha's left. Her stomach sank—it was the small boy from before. He tried to freeze back into position, but it was too late.

"Ah, the runt," Sealy said. "Think you got what it takes to serve our lady?"

The boy looked at the ground and shook his head.

"What's wrong, boy? Can't talk?" He leaned closer to the child, who was shaking in his small brown loafers. "You even think about not speaking when Lord Faisel addresses you, and he'll make you a permanent mute."

The boy uttered a weak, "Yes, sir."

"Are you even strong enough to carry a tray?" Sealy poked the boy in the shoulder, causing him to stumble backward. "If you spill so much as one drop of my—"

"I will volunteer," Tasha said. She took a step forward, hoping that she wouldn't trip over her clumsy feet. "I would be honored to serve the lady," Tasha said.

Sealy marched to her. "Think you got what it takes, blondie?"

Tasha willed herself not to back down. "I know I do, sir," she said.

"Well, you've got guts." Sealy smirked. "But Lord Faisel isn't afraid to cut those out of kids as well."

Tasha didn't respond to Sealy's horrible joke. She wasn't some county girl from Stetriol anymore. She was a Greencloak. Or, a Greencloak-in-training. Or, whatever. All she knew was that she couldn't stand there and watch that boy get bullied.

"So, it's you and the runt, then."

"I'd like to volunteer as well."

Tasha sighed. *Rollan.*

Sealy walked to Rollan. "I don't need three of you," he said.

"I'll go in his place," Rollan said, nodding to the boy.

Sealy poked Rollan hard in the chest. Rollan must have been anticipating it, because his feet somehow remained in place, and his body didn't bend. "At least you look like you could carry a tray of food." Sealy pointed toward two large platters, each stacked with food, then rattled off directions. "And don't drop those plates," he added as Tasha and Rollan exited the kitchen.

Tasha remained quiet as she followed Rollan down the corridor. He was walking too quickly for her to catch up and see his face. Was he so upset with her that he couldn't even talk?

Finally, she said, "I know you're mad. I'm sorry. I'm just . . . I don't like bullies."

Rollan stopped walking. His eyes were too blank for Tasha to read. "Yeah, what you did was a little crazy," he said. "But you did the right thing."

"So you're not mad? I thought, since you weren't saying anything–"

He shook his head. "No, I was thinking about what Meilin would have done. She doesn't like bullies, either. Remind me to tell you about how she jumped into shark-infested waters to save some whales."

There it was again—that sadness. While she could often feel Ninani enhancing her powers of perception, she didn't need the Great Beast's help to see this.

"I'm sure she's okay," Tasha said. "From what I've heard, she's one of the Greencloaks' finest warriors."

Rollan nodded. "If by finest you mean most stubborn, then yes, you're correct." He regripped his tray, and they continued walking. "Plus, do you know how big this place is? If we were on cleaning duty, we'd be mopping all day."

They continued down another long corridor before coming to a grand dining hall. Tasha cautiously entered the room. Large, multicolored tapestries hung from the ceiling to the floor of each wall. She had known many weavers in Stetriol, and knew that it would have taken them months to create artwork so exquisite.

Tasha took a few more steps into the room. "Hello?" she called out.

"Please, come in," a woman said. Tasha hadn't seen her before she spoke. The woman wore a loose, flowing red dress, causing her to almost blend in with the room's satin curtains. She moved away from the window. "I'm LaReimaja," she said. "You must be the new servants Faisel hired. You may put those on the table."

Tasha started to move forward, then suddenly went flying. She tried to grab the plates on her tray as she fell, which only caused her to land even harder on the woven rug.

Rollan rushed to her. "Tasha?" he whispered.

"I'm fine," she said. Most of her plates had over-turned, spilling dates, grains, and slices of bread on the floor. Luckily, none of the dishes had broken. Then she noticed the overturned bowl of butter she had been carrying. She crawled to it and flipped it over. The soft butter had already begun to seep into the carpet.

"Oh no," she moaned as she tried to sop it up with the edge of her dress.

"My dear, it's okay," LaReimaja said as she knelt beside Tasha. The lady pointed to Rollan. "There are some towels in the adjacent room," she said to him.

As Rollan ran off, Tasha dared to look at the woman. Lady LaReimaja was very beautiful, with warm features and dark tan skin. Her friendly eyes were the color of coffee, a drink that the Greencloaks had brought with them to Stetriol and which smelled to Tasha like earth and honey. "I'm am so, so sorry," Tasha began. "Your carpet—"

"—is just that. Only a carpet." LaReimaja began picking up the scattered food. Then she paused and placed her hands against one of the green-and-yellow floral designs woven into the rug. "With as much time as I spend in this room, I tend to forget that this carpet is even here." She patted it. "It's one of my favorites. I made it years ago. Another lifetime."

Rollan returned with a few towels in his hands. He hesitated once he reached them, his eyes on LaReimaja. "Will these work?" he finally asked.

"Thank you. These will be fine," LaReimaja said, taking one of the towels. She began blotting the carpet where the soft butter had spilled. "Why don't you try to wipe up that jam?" she said to Rollan.

Rollan moved to another part of the carpet and did

as he was instructed, but Tasha noticed how, every so often, he would turn and gaze at the woman, each glance longer than the one before. It was as if he was searching her face for something.

Maybe LaReimaja reminded him of his mother. Tasha certainly felt that way. As they worked together to clean up the mess, Tasha thought back to how she and her mother would work together to clean the house while her father traveled from village to village, taking care of people's horses.

She hoped that she would see her parents again, and that they were safe.

Tasha noticed that LaReimaja had cleaned up all the butter and was now patting the carpet again.

"It's really beautiful," Tasha said, touching the carpet as well. "Did you also create the tapestries?"

LaReimaja nodded. "I probably knew how to weave before I could walk. My family owned a carpet shop in the market—my siblings and I would weave the carpets at night and sell them during the day. But after marrying Faisel, I no longer had to make carpets for profit. I could truly engage in the art of loommanship." She sighed. "However, there are only so many tapestries you can weave before even that becomes mundane."

Tasha returned to scooping up the grain. She had almost finished when a large, bearded man entered the room. "What is this?" he demanded.

LaReimaja quickly rose to her feet. Tasha started to get up, but LaReimaja nudged her back to the carpet. "It's nothing, Faisel," she said, dropping the towel.

"Did these servants—"

"It was my fault," she said as she rushed to her husband. "I wasn't paying attention to where I was walking. I collided with the girl and caused her to spill everything." She took Faisel's arm and led him to the table. "But there is plenty of food on the other tray if you would like to eat."

"I have more things to worry about than food," he said, shaking her arm away. "Our guests begin arriving tonight, and your son still can't control his spirit animal."

"Cabaro isn't any ordinary spirit animal," LaReimaja said. "And I don't think the connection works like that. It's a partnership—"

"If I didn't know any better, I would say that you sound like a Greencloak." He picked up a date and bit into it. "I've doubled the guards. There's no way that Dante and his band of Greencloaks are getting inside this castle."

Tasha had finished cleaning up the food near her, but didn't dare move to a different location. A few paces away, Rollan pretended to clean the same spot in the carpet, over and over again.

"I know you don't favor the Greencloaks, but they may be able to help Kirat," LaReimaja said as she offered Faisel another date. "They cannot be any worse than all those advisers you hired."

"Well, you're right about that—those *experts* are useless. I've already dismissed most of them." He picked up another date. At this rate, Tasha assumed there would be nothing left for LaReimaja to eat. "But an interesting thing happened during Kirat's breakfast. One of the servants actually stood up to Cabaro. And the lion backed down."

"Who? Was it Ahmar?"

Faisel smiled, causing a tremor to run through Tasha's body. He reminded her of the Reptile King's crocodile. She had seen it once, from afar, during the war. "No, it was one of the new servants. A girl with braids—probably from the savannahs, by the look of her."

Tasha and Rollan looked at each other. *Abeke.*

LaReimaja sighed. "Faisel, you promised not to expose the younger servants to Cabaro. Remember what happened to the milk girl?"

Faisel shrugged. "It's just some village girl. Better for her to lose a few fingers than one of my staff." He picked up the last of the dates, then walked toward the door. He paused before exiting. "LaReimaja, make sure those servants clean that carpet so it's spotless. I would hate for someone else to lose a few fingers."

ADRIFT

L IKE IT HAD BEEN YESTERDAY, AND THE DAY BEFORE, and perhaps even the day before that, the water surrounding their small boat was still, dark, and quiet.

Conor couldn't go to sleep.

He was bone tired, and the many days of remaining so inactive in the boat had made his muscles loose, almost as if they were beginning to forget how to work. He knew that if he slept, he would be able to escape from the dryness in his mouth and the ache in his stomach, at least for a little while.

But every time Conor began to drift off to sleep, he could feel the Wyrm probing his mind. Trying to control him. The whispers had grown louder. And his dreams, once filled with images from the green fields of Trunswick, were now dark and troubling. When he closed his eyes, he still returned to his homeland, but the once-green grass was now dead and brown. Trees and fences were stained with blood. A battle raged throughout the town, with him and the Many on one side, and his friends on the other. And his friends were losing.

Briggan nudged his leg, pulling him out of his current thoughts. He scratched the wolf's muzzle. Conor knew he should put Briggan into his passive state. He was the only animal on the boat—even Kovo had agreed to return to the tattoo on Takoda's neck once they realized that he could no longer help with the rowing. Conor had found a few scraps of leathery, stale jerky deep in his pockets, but that was almost gone. Soon, all that would be left was the rockweed. He wasn't sure if Briggan would even eat it.

He thought about searching through their meager supplies to find something—anything—for Briggan to eat, but he would have to depend more on touch than sight, and that would wake everyone up.

They were down to their last wooden torch. The two glowing spheres that Takoda had found in the caves had already dulled from warm green to dark brown. And the orb that had been attached to the anglerfish had gone dark only a few moments after being separated from the fish.

Conor knew that Meilin felt responsible for everything that had happened during the attack. They had lost their paddle and were now at the mercy of the current. Conor still believed they would make it to the Evertree—eventually. The current seemed to be slowly pulling them in the direction of the Wyrm. He just hoped he could hold on to his sanity until then.

And then what? he wondered. How were they going to defeat the Wyrm? They could barely escape an anglerfish.

Briggan nudged his leg again. "I'm sorry, was I drifting again?" he asked. Then he looked at Briggan, his ears sitting straight up on his head, the fur on his neck stiff.

"What is it?" Conor asked.

Briggan looked at Conor, then turned his attention back to whatever was out there. Conor calmed himself and tried to push away everything clogging his mind. Eventually, he found Briggan in the abyss and tapped into his power. The world became even quieter for a second, and then he heard it. Talking. No . . . singing.

Someone was out there on the water.

"Wake up, guys!" Conor yelled. He shook Meilin and then Takoda. "Do you hear that? It's singing." He pointed. "It's coming from that way."

Meilin shook her head, causing her black hair to cascade over her eyes. "I don't hear anything."

"Me neither," Takoda said.

"I couldn't either, not at first," Conor said. "But Briggan is helping to enhance my senses." He rubbed the wolf's flank. "You hear it, too, right?"

The wolf howled, then nodded. He shakily rose from the belly of the boat, padded to the edge, and pointed his snout in the same direction that Conor had indicated.

Meilin began pulling her hair into a ponytail. "It could just be the wind," she said. "Or worse, another strange animal intent on killing us."

"No," Conor said. "I hear words." He went silent and let himself tap into Briggan's hearing. "I'm positive. It's a group of people singing."

Takoda pursed his lips together as he studied Conor. It was clear that Takoda was focusing on the black mark making its way up Conor's neck.

"It's not the parasite or the Wyrm," Conor added defiantly. "I'm sure." But was he? How could he even trust his senses?

"Well, even if it is singing, there isn't much we can do about it," Takoda said. "It's not like we can paddle ourselves to them."

Meilin shifted her body and crossed her arms. Conor knew that Takoda hadn't been trying to scold or blame Meilin, but she clearly took it that way.

"We have one other option," Conor said. "We can light the last torch."

Takoda rubbed his jaw. "I don't know, Conor. It's not that I don't trust you—"

"Then what is it?" Conor asked, his voice hard.

"What if you're wrong?" Takoda asked. "We might use our last torch, and then be totally in the dark."

"We're running out of food," Conor said. *And out of time*, he almost added. "Those people out there could help us."

"Or they could be our enemy," Meilin said. She slowly stood and moved closer to the two boys. "Or we could light the torch and go unnoticed, and we would be right back in the same position, except without any other light." Meilin scratched the tattoo on the back of her hand. "Jhi enhances my abilities in many ways, but not in hearing or sight," she said. "Does Kovo?"

Takoda shook his head. "No. At least not yet. But there's much about our bond that I still don't understand."

Meilin looked into Conor's eyes. "Are you sure about this?"

"I think it's our best chance," Conor said.

"Then that's good enough for me," Meilin said. "Takoda?"

He exhaled long and hard, before finally nodding. "I don't agree, but I'll defer to your wisdom." He picked up the torch and handed it to Conor. "You're the tallest. You give us the best chance of being seen."

"We should tie it to my quarterstaff with some rope," Meilin said. She began rummaging through the boat. "That will get it even higher."

Once they'd lashed the torch onto the staff, Conor lit it and hoisted it high above his head.

"I would call Kovo to hold it," Takoda said, "but I'm afraid that he would just put it out. He's . . . not your biggest fan. I don't know if he would believe you."

"Are you talking about me or Conor?" Meilin asked.

"Um, both of you," he replied.

Conor tried to ignore their banter, and instead focused on holding the torch high above his head. He tried to wave it a few times, but after almost dropping it, he decided it would be best to hold it still. But his hands were slippery with sweat, and his shoulders ached. He wasn't sure how much longer he could keep it raised.

Suddenly, Jhi appeared beside Conor. "Please help him, Jhi," Meilin said. "Conor needs all his concentration to keep the staff still and high."

Conor immediately felt his heart rate slow down. His arms burned, but not nearly as much. The panda had placed her body right beside Conor, causing everything else to fade away to the background.

Conor looked up. The torch, once blazing bright, had

begun to die down. He still hadn't seen any response from the dark sea. The singing seemed to have stopped, but Conor didn't know if that was because Jhi was suppressing the outside world, helping Conor focus on the here and now.

Then, finally, a blue light ignited far in the distance. Then another, and a third after that. Jhi pulled away from him, and the real world came rushing back.

"I think they see us," Meilin said. She took the staff from Conor. "And now, we wait."

THE *MELEAGER*

CONOR WAS THE FIRST TO SEE THE SMALL SKIFF MAKING its way through the water to them. All Takoda and Meilin could see was a blue glowstone slowly floating through the darkness. For all Takoda knew, it was another anglerfish and not a boat. But perhaps none of that mattered anymore. Whatever it was, it was on its way, and there was nothing that Takoda and the others could do about it anymore.

Takoda picked up his cloak and fastened it around his shoulders. He pulled it high in order to hide Kovo's mark on his neck. "They'll be here soon. You should probably ask your spirit animals to return to passive form then."

Meilin leaned over and stared Jhi in the eyes. A second later, she disappeared.

"Conor, did you hear me?" Takoda asked.

Conor looked at Briggan, then at Meilin. "Don't let me fall asleep before releasing him," Conor said.

Meilin frowned. "Conor, nothing is going to happen—"

"Just promise me!" he yelled, his face becoming twisted and angry. He kicked out at a random bag—the one containing what remained of their rockweed. Takoda yelped and caught it just before it went over the edge of the boat.

Meilin held her hands up in front of her. "Conor, you have to calm down," she said, her voice barely audible over the sound of water lapping against the boat. "You're rocking the boat too much. Look at Briggan."

The wolf's legs wobbled underneath him as he tried to position himself between Conor and Meilin. Briggan whimpered, but kept moving until he had blocked Conor from her.

Conor blinked, and his blue eyes returned to normal. "I'm . . . I'm so sorry." He hid his face in his hands. "What's happening to me?"

Meilin placed her hand on Conor's shoulder. "Just ask Briggan to return to his dormant state," she said. "He won't do it if he doesn't trust you."

Conor nodded. Seconds later, the Great Wolf vanished in a flash.

"See," Meilin said. "Briggan believes in you, and so do I. You can beat this, Conor."

Instead of answering, Conor retreated to the far side of the boat, away from Meilin and Takoda.

Takoda stepped toward Meilin as she continued to pack their supplies. "The ship will be here soon," Takoda said. "It would be nice to get a real meal. You know, something better than rockweed. Maybe even something warm. Or sweet." He cast another look at Conor, who was silently staring off into the sea. "It will also give us a chance to rest and restock our supplies.

We have to be at full strength in order to face what's ahead."

Meilin stopped packing the bag. "Takoda, cut the small talk. Neither of us have the time or energy to tip-toe around whatever's on your mind. Just say it, and let's get this over with."

Takoda felt his face warm. He wasn't used to some-one being so blunt. The monks, while direct, often found a way to soften their displeasure with their tone and choice of words. That was *not* Meilin's way.

"Conor isn't getting better," Takoda whispered. "You remember what Xanthe said. They weren't able to save any of the Many."

"He will be different."

"Meilin—"

"You worry about keeping Kovo in line. I'll take care of Conor," she said. "Now, are we done?" she asked, starting to move away. "The ship will be here soon."

Takoda slid in front of her, blocking her path. "I promise I'm not trying to be difficult. I *am* hoping for the best for Conor. But we need a contingency plan."

Meilin's eyes narrowed. She picked up her quarter-staff and spun it in her hands. "As I said, I will take care of Conor. One way or another. Understood?"

Takoda nodded and stepped out of her way. Their confrontation was just another example of how she reminded him of Kovo. Both were willing to do what they felt was necessary, perhaps even at the sake of their own souls. He couldn't imagine attacking one of the monks from his monastery. But Kovo had battled the other Great Beasts because he believed he was right and they were wrong. And now, Meilin was willing to face her friend if Conor eventually turned. Would Takoda ever be as brave as them?

He finished packing his belongings, then joined Meilin and Conor at the starboard side of the boat.

Across the yellow sea, the skiff was now close enough for him to see it. Oars moved in sync as they sliced through the water. In. Out. Up. Down. Back. Forth.

"One thing is certain," Meilin said. "They aren't infected. There's no way that the Many would be so organized."

The strangers' glowstone went dark as the skiff came to a stop. Takoda could make out faint humanoid silhouettes on the boat—it almost looked like the people were blue-skinned. A horn blew in the distance. "Identify yourselves," someone yelled from the skiff. "What city do you hail from?"

Meilin pointed to herself, and Takoda nodded in agreement. Then she leaned forward. "We are travelers, new to this land," she yelled, her voice sounding much stronger than her slight build would have indicated. "We became adrift in the Sulfur Sea and have been at the mercy of the currents ever since." She looked at Conor. "We would be grateful for any assistance."

"And what can you offer us in return for our help?" the person on the other ship replied.

Meilin covered her mouth. "Great," she whispered. "Pirates." She turned back toward the ship and cupped her hands around her mouth. "We don't have anything of value on hand, but if you take us aboard your vessel and give us safe passage, we'll find a means to compensate you."

"In other words, you have nothing to pay or barter!"

"No! We have considerable wealth," Meilin said. "It just . . . isn't here."

"And where is it? At the bottom of the sea?" Takoda thought he heard laughter from the pirate boat. "Unless you own gills, your treasure is now useless to you."

Takoda leaned over toward Meilin. "The truth?" he whispered.

Meilin shrugged, then nodded. "It's . . . aboveground," she yelled. "We are from Erdas."

Silence passed between the two boats for a few minutes. Takoda was not a fighter, but he would have felt more at ease with a weapon in his hand.

The boat began moving again, and the skiff's glowstone was reignited. Takoda realized that a young woman was holding the orb. She moved to the bow of the pirates' boat. Takoda had never seen a pirate before, but he had heard countless stories about them at the monastery. They were described as rough, unkempt, and untrustworthy, usually covered in dirt and grime. The worst stories always featured a captain with rotting teeth, a peg for a leg, and a hook for an arm.

This pirate looked nothing like that. Her gray coat and trousers were neat, perhaps even pressed. Her pale hair was covered with a bandanna, with a single braid hanging over her shoulder. Her sleeves were rolled up to her elbows. A network of small blue veins snaked up her pale arms.

"I am Teutar, first mate of the mighty *Meleager*." She held up the light and peered at them. "So, this is what uplanders look like."

Takoda didn't respond. He wasn't sure if she was really asking them a question or not.

"Is it only you three?"

They nodded.

"Grab your gear and climb aboard," she said. "We're not usually in the business of taking stowaways, but our captain has always been the curious type. You can take up your request for safe passage with her."

The pirates maneuvered the boat next to them. Meilin stepped on first, followed by Conor and Takoda. The skiff was full, with two pirates to a seat. Takoda realized that they were all women.

Yet another thing to readjust to. In the stories he'd heard at the monastery, the pirates had always been large, bearded men.

Takoda also noticed that all the pirates had a patchwork of blue veins crisscrossing their arms. Some even spread to their necks.

"Like 'em?" Teutar asked. She flexed her arm, and the blue began to glow. Takoda then realized that they weren't veins, but instead a series of intricate, swirling tattoos. "We use special ink to make them light up when we want them to," she said. "Bet you've never seen a fancy tattoo like this aboveground, have you?"

Takoda forced himself to keep his face passive and emotionless. "Yes, very impressive." He wondered if he would have a chance to show off *his* tattoo.

Slowly, the pirates' ship came into view. He had thought that the *Tellun's Pride II* was massive, but it was nothing compared to the pirates' vessel. It contained three masts, all reaching so high that they seemed to puncture the blackness above. Cannons sat along the edge of the ship, each seemingly large enough for Takoda and Kovo to climb into, with room to spare.

"Welcome to the *Meleager*," Teutar said. The crew navigated themselves alongside the ship, where a few ropes hung from above. They attached the ropes to the skiff and were hoisted up.

Takoda tried to ignore all the eyes on him as he stepped onto the deck of the *Meleager*. He pulled the collar of his cloak tighter around his neck and moved forward.

"Where's the captain?" Teutar asked once the last of the crew had exited the skiff. "She will want to meet these three immediately."

Slowly, the group of pirates shifted and parted. A tall and wiry woman stepped from the crowd. Like the others, her arms and legs were covered in blue tattoos. But hers seemed to be alive, swirling and moving as she walked toward them. "I am Atalanta, captain of the *Meleager*." She pulled a cutlass from her side. "Who are you?" Then she frowned. "No. *What* are you?"

Teutar stepped forward. "They're upsiders," she said, her voice now much more quiet.

"Impossible!" the captain replied. The tattoos on her arm lit up and began to swirl furiously.

"It's true," Meilin said. She made a small bow toward the woman. Takoda and Conor quickly did the same. "We are from above," Meilin continued. "We were exploring a cave when it collapsed. We've been stuck underground ever since."

Technically not a lie, Takoda thought.

"And how did you come to find the Sulfur Sea?" the captain asked.

"We had a guide—a girl from Phos Astos," Meilin

replied. "But as we crossed the Arachane Fields, we became separated. With no guide to lead us, we finally decided to take to the sea, but lost our oars during an attack from a large anglerfish."

Atalanta nodded. "Good thing you didn't try to get into the water. They don't like *our* flesh—the ink helps to keep them away—but I bet they would have found you plenty tasty." The tattoos on her arms stilled and returned to their normal, dull blue. "So, what's it like up above?" She circled them, then poked Takoda's shoulder. "Are they all small like you?"

"We come in all sizes, shapes, and colors," Takoda said. "We would be honored to tell you more about the land above . . . perhaps over a meal?"

Atalanta laughed. "Stories for food? Hmm, not quite as profitable as gold or equipment, but I do love a good story." She slapped him on the shoulder, almost causing Takoda's legs to buckle. "Come. Tell me your tales. If I'm impressed, I won't throw you overboard." Although she was smiling when she said it, Takoda wasn't sure if her comment was a joke or a real threat.

As they fell into step behind the captain and her first mate, Meilin grabbed Takoda's arm. "Please tell me you have something impressive to share. Something more exciting than sitting on a hillside in blue robes and chanting."

He smiled. "We do more than chant," he said. "And not all of us wear blue robes. Saffron is just as popular." He waited for Meilin to smile at his joke. When she didn't, he said, "Don't worry. I think I have a tale that will be exciting enough for our new friends. That is, unless you would like to tell the first story. Perhaps something from Zhong, or from the war?"

Something flashed in her eyes, as if she was remembering a painful memory. "Some stories don't deserve to be celebrated."

"But it's through stories that we remember those who came before us," he said. "It's how we honor the fallen."

She shrugged. "Perhaps. But not today." She hesitated, then said, "But ask me again later, and I'll tell you my father's story. He was a great general, a noble warrior, and a wonderful father. And then maybe you'll tell me more about your parents, too?"

"It's a deal," Takoda said.

She quickly moved away from him to join Conor. When Takoda had learned of the Four Heroes of Erdas, he had only heard stories about Meilin in battle. Of how, even at such a young age, she was one of the Greencloaks' greatest warriors. He'd spent so much time thinking about his own parents, he didn't stop to consider that others—even the Heroes of Erdas—had lost loved ones during the war.

Meilin's father had paid the ultimate price. And now, so had Xanthe.

Takoda followed Atalanta, Teutar, and a small group of pirates into a windowless room. Blue orbs hung from the ceiling, casting out faint amounts of light. Even with the orbs, it took Takoda a few moments for his eyes to adjust. Then he noticed the table. This must have been where they dined. Atalanta sat down first. The rest of the crew took seats around her. She pointed to a few chairs. "Sit," she said. "You're lucky. Our cook just whipped up a batch of brinefish and mushrooms. Let's see how you uplanders do with a real Sadrean meal." Then she pointed to Takoda. "Now, where is my story?"

Takoda remained standing while the others sat down. It was how the monks in the order all told stories, and it would have felt uncomfortable to do otherwise. After thinking for a few moments, he decided to tell the story about the founder of their monastery, a great soldier who eventually tired of war, sold his possessions, and began their order. Takoda considered embellishing certain parts, especially the portion of their founder's time as a mercenary, but quickly changed his mind. It was one thing to stretch the truth, but something else entirely to lie about it. It felt disrespectful to both himself and the founder.

As he talked, Atalanta, Teutar, and the other members of the crew cheered at all the parts of the story about war and battle, which he had expected. However, the crew became quiet and contemplative at the redemptive parts of the tale, which greatly surprised Takoda. These pirates were nothing like the stories he had heard at the monastery.

Platters of food continued to be served as he talked. Everyone, including his friends, were able to eat as much as they wanted. Takoda noticed Meilin slipping slices of meat and bread into her bag, hopefully for their spirit animals.

Once Takoda finished his story, he sat down and loaded food onto his own plate. After eating nothing but rockweed for the past few days, the dried, leathery fish and slimy mushrooms tasted like the best of Niloan desserts. He ate quickly and asked for a second plate.

Meilin leaned into Takoda. "Eat fast," she whispered. "We don't have much time." Then she nodded toward Conor. His forehead was covered in sweat. He had only eaten half of his food, and was now staring at the wall.

"He needs to rest," Takoda said. "Perhaps Jhi—"

"There isn't much more she can do for him," Meilin said. "Stopping the Wyrm is the only way to save him now."

Takoda quickly ate a few pieces of fish from his second plate, then slipped the rest of the food into his pockets. "Thank you, Captain," he said. "The meal was excellent."

"As was the story," she said. She stabbed a piece of fish with her knife. "Perhaps now you all will tell me the real reason you were adrift on the Sulfur Sea," she said before popping the fish into her mouth.

The room went quiet as the pirates heard this. Every head turned, focused on the three uplanders.

Meilin slowly pushed her plate away. "You're correct. We didn't travel this way by chance. We came in search of the Evertree."

A few of the pirates began to murmur, but Atalanta motioned for them to be quiet. "I assumed as much," she said. "Congratulations on surviving the Arachane Fields and the Sulfur Sea. I applaud your bravery. A lesser group would have turned back."

"So will you take us there?" Takoda asked.

Atalanta shook her head. "My friends, there is no profit in that. Only death."

"But surely you have encountered the Many," Meilin said. "The Evertree is sick, and the Wyrm is growing stronger with each passing moment. If we don't find a way to defeat it, both of our worlds will be destroyed." She looked at each of the pirates at the table. "Phos Astos has fallen. For all we know, you may be the last of your people."

Atalanta sat back in her chair. "What proof do you have that this is true?"

"We were there," Takoda said. "They fought bravely, but fell quickly. In less than an hour, the city was completely overwhelmed by the Many."

The captain let out a long sigh. "And you say this is all tied to the Evertree?"

Teutar leaned toward Atalanta and banged her fist against the table. "You surely can't be considering taking them—"

"The last time I checked, I was the captain of this vessel. Not you or anyone else." Atalanta rose from her seat. "Come. Enough talk of this for today. You should rest. We will discuss what to do with you tomorrow."

Meilin and Takoda quickly stood from their seats, while Conor struggled to push himself away from the table.

"What's wrong with this one?" one of the pirates asked, walking toward Conor. She took a swig of her drink and wiped her mouth with the back of her hand. "Ate too much fish?"

Takoda rushed around the table to help Conor, but the pirate had already reached him. She took him by the arm and easily yanked him to his feet. Then she dropped her mug and stumbled away him. "He's been infected!"

Takoda stepped between Conor and the pirate.

Meilin joined him a second later. "He's fine," she said.

"You brought one of the infected onto my ship?" Atalanta yelled. Her tattoos swirled over her skin, casting the entire room in an ethereal blue glow. "You must kill him. Now."

"Not going to happen," Meilin said, tightening her grip on her quarterstaff.

"Friend, I wasn't asking," Atalanta said. In a flash, an enormous bullfrog appeared at her side. It was easily as large as Jhi. The bullfrog flicked its tongue like a whip. It circled Meilin's staff and then yanked it away.

"You aren't the only one with a spirit animal," Takoda said, pulling back his cloak.

Instantly, Kovo appeared. He let out a loud, deafening roar, causing all the pirates to step backward. The ape picked up two chairs and flung them at the nearest of the crew. One was able to duck in time, but the other fell into a slump as the chair exploded against her.

"Get help!" Teutar said to one of the pirates. Then she drew her sword and advanced.

"We won't be able to fight them all," Takoda said.

Kovo roared again, then picked up a large wooden table and swung it like a club, taking out two more attackers. Most of the others had wisely backed up, remaining outside of Kovo's swing.

Most . . . but not all. Teutar timed her advance perfectly, ducking underneath the table and rushing toward the group. Meilin picked up a chair and blocked her thrust before it could connect. Teutar continued to cut away at the chair, slice by slice. Meilin was down to holding the leg when Takoda felt a rush of hot air beside him. Then Briggan leaped into the air, landing beside Teutar. The wolf bit into her arm, and Teutar screamed in pain, lowering her sword. That gave Meilin enough of an opening to strike. A flurry of rapid blows that were almost too fast to see sent Teutar tumbling backward into the row of pirates.

Kovo stepped between them, now holding the table like a shield.

Takoda pointed to the door behind them. It was the only way out of the room. With the pirates between them and the door, there was no way to escape . . . but maybe they could force the pirates out.

"The door!" Takoda yelled. "Push them out!"

Kovo lumbered toward the ship's crew with a menacing grin, looking more than pleased with this plan. The last pirate had just scrambled out of the room before the enormous gorilla rammed the table into the doorway, effectively barricading it. The pirates yelled from the other side, but they couldn't get into the room—at least for the time being.

Takoda glanced at Conor as he began tying up one of the unconscious pirates with a length of rope. "Didn't know if I was going to be able to call Briggan. The bond is so weak, and my head feels really foggy. It's like everything is out of focus." Conor paused to wipe the sweat from his brow. "I can't put him back into passive."

"We have bigger problems than that," Meilin said. "We're stuck in a room with no way out, and an army of pirates between us and the nearest boat." She picked up her quarterstaff. "I hope Atalanta is the only one with a spirit animal."

Then something very loud, and very large, rammed into the door. The table scooted back, but Kovo quickly smashed it back into place. Atalanta's bullfrog croaked from the other side, and the door didn't move again.

"I hope that frog is all right," Takoda said, wincing.

"Speak for yourself," Meilin said. She quickly surveyed the room. "At least the crew left some of their weapons in here before they retreated." She placed her quarterstaff on the table, then picked up a sword that had been dropped. She tried to hand it to Takoda, but he shook his head.

"I've never used a sword before."

"Well, there's a first time for everything," Meilin replied. Jhi appeared a moment later in a flash of light. She looked around before finding Conor, then lumbered over to him and began licking his face.

"Jhi hasn't given up on him," Meilin said to Takoda. She pushed the sword into his hand, and this time he took it. "And as long as he fights, so will we."

12

CONFRONTING KIRAT

IT WAS STILL DARK WHEN ABEKE WOKE. SHE TOOK A FEW deep breaths and tried to slow her rapidly beating heart. She had been dreaming. She was in Okaihee with her father and sister. She and her sister had just returned from collecting water from the river when Rumfuss the Boar charged into the hut, destroying it. Abeke released Uraza. The Great Beasts squared off while she grabbed her bow and collected her arrows. Then Dinesh appeared, followed by Suka and Tellun. Her father launched a spear into the elephant's side, but that only seemed to make the animal angrier. Dinesh charged at them, but they were able to dodge the elephant's ivory tusks. They escaped from the hut, with Abeke taking the lead.

She stopped once they reached the edge of their village. That's when she noticed the black swirls on her father's and sister's foreheads. She loaded her bow and arrow and warned them to stay where they were. They charged her anyway, their eyes blank.

Then she woke up. Thankfully.

Abeke slipped out of bed and placed her bare feet on the cool floor. Then, after a few seconds of concentration, she released Uraza. Even with Uraza just a few steps from her, Abeke could hardly feel their bond. She rubbed Uraza's spotted flank and immediately felt calmer. They would find a way through this. Together.

After a few seconds, the leopard left Abeke's side and slinked toward the door.

"I'm sorry, girl," Abeke said as Uraza pawed the wooden door. "You know I can't be seen with you. There's only one Uraza the Leopard, and she isn't bonded to a serving girl."

She pulled a few strips of bacon from her bag and tossed three to Uraza. It had been easy to pilfer the food from one of the discarded plates that Kirat had barely touched. Abeke had to struggle to hold her temper every time Kirat picked at his food and then cast it away, barely eaten. She had seen enough food wasted to last her village for an entire season. And it wasn't just the horrible-tasting food that he had cast aside—it was desserts! Custard and cakes and honey-covered biscuits. She didn't care how much wealth she had, she would never pass up a lemon custard.

Abeke held out another rasher of bacon for Uraza, but instead of letting it go, she used it to play tug-of-war. Uraza played along for a while, growling and grunting at her. But eventually, Uraza released the bacon, causing Abeke to fly backward into the legs of Rollan's bed.

"Hey, some of us are trying to sleep here," Rollan

grumbled, his eyes still closed. "Watch where you're walking, Tasha."

Abeke took the bacon and tapped the wet end against Rollan's ear. His eyes flashed open. "You don't have to blame everything on Tasha," she said.

"Yeah," Tasha added. She tried to rise from bed, but her blanket was still twisted around her legs, causing her to tumble.

Rollan rolled his eyes. "What were you saying?"

Abeke smiled. "Well, since you're awake, you might as well get up," she said. "It will be light soon. You don't want to miss breakfast."

"Maybe we could skip," Tasha said as she began braiding her hair. "LaReimaja is so nice, I'll bet she would let us eat some of her leftovers."

"I wish," Rollan said. "Could you imagine the trouble we'd be in if Faisel walked in on us scarfing down one of those sticky buns?"

"It may be worth taking a chance, if Sealy prepares the same mush that he tried to force on us yesterday," Tasha said. Then she started humming to herself.

Rollan sat up with a startled expression, his back as straight as Zourtzi's walls. "What are you singing?"

Tasha finished her braid. "Just something I heard LaReimaja singing to herself yesterday during her lunch, when she was trying to convince herself to try Sealy's monkey eyeball soup." She shrugged as she looked at Abeke. "Supposedly, it's a delicacy in the Kaisung Mountains."

"If I can, I'll try to retrieve some of Kirat's leftovers," Abeke said.

"No thanks," Rollan said. "I don't want a spoiled rich kid's hand-me-downs."

Tasha cleared her throat. "Um, I wouldn't mind some plums."

"Plums for one, it is." Abeke scratched Uraza's belly. The leopard stretched out, splaying her claws, and purred softly. "Hopefully I'll find some time to speak to Kirat, without his advisers or father hovering around."

"Have you figured out how you're going to get him to come along?" Rollan asked.

Abeke shook her head. "Outside of force . . . I'm unsure. Do you think you could speak to Faisel's wife about it? If she's as understanding as you and Tasha claim she is, maybe she could be an ally."

Rollan rubbed his jaw. "Maybe. Faisel's hatred of Greencloaks runs deep, but LaReimaja seems more even-tempered about us. She even understands how the bond works between us and our spirit animals."

"Do you think she has a spirit animal?" Abeke asked. After Tasha and Rollan shook their heads, Abeke rose to her feet. "Well, I should get moving. Faisel wants his son's breakfast delivered early this morning. He's taking Kirat gazelle hunting with some of his guests." Abeke smiled. "Maybe that'll get Cabaro to move, and at least act like a lion. Usually he just lays there and waits for me to place his food before him."

"That doesn't surprise me. His laziness transcended even death," Rollan said. "Knowing Cabaro, he only picked you because he likes the idea of you and Uraza waiting on him hand and foot."

Uraza growled, seemingly in agreement.

"Hush, Uraza. Not you, too!" Abeke said. "I don't even know if Cabaro remembers me. I only saw him once, at the Evertree."

A scowl spread across Rollan's face. "Consider yourself lucky."

Abeke tossed the last piece of bacon to Uraza. She didn't like to see her friend like this, so angry and sullen. She knew he was cranky because he was worried about Meilin, but it was clear there was more to it.

She knelt in front of Rollan. "I wasn't with you when Tarik and Lumeo fell. I know how–"

Rollan fiercely shook his head. "I don't want to talk about it."

"I understand." She patted his hand. "But if you do, you know you can."

He looked at the floor for a long time, not speaking. Finally, he nodded, mumbled an acknowledgment of Abeke's comment, then walked to the window.

Tasha cleared her throat again. "So, how about that breakfast?"

"There's one other option we should talk about before we leave," Rollan said, still staring out the window. "Maybe we *shouldn't* try to take Kirat."

"Zerif will eventually come for him," Abeke said.

"But can he *get* to him?" Rollan asked, turning around to face her. "You've both seen how protected this castle is. If Zourtzi was strong enough to keep the Conquerors at bay during the war, then perhaps it could keep Zerif out, too. It's at least worth considering." Rollan glanced at Tasha. "And maybe Kirat's not the only one who should remain."

Tasha's hands balled into fists. "You want me to stay

here?" she asked, her voice rising. "I know I'm a little clumsy, but I deserve a chance to fight for Erdas, like you and Abeke."

"The best thing you can do for Erdas is to keep Ninani safe," Rollan said. "And that might mean staying here. I'm sure if we explained it to LaReimaja, she would find a way to keep you within the fortress."

"And what about you and Abeke?" Tasha demanded. "Will you remain in Zourtzi as well?"

"We can't," Rollan said. "But perhaps, when Dante gets well he can stay with you and—"

"Enough," Abeke said. "None of us are staying here." Abeke moved to the center of the room and crossed her arms. Uraza stood beside her. She didn't want to come across as taking over—they were a team, and everyone deserved to have a say. But she also knew that she had to keep them focused on their mission. She looked squarely at Rollan. "I may not know Cabaro, but I know Zerif. I've seen his methods up close. Trust me, he will come, and he will take Cabaro and any other spirit animal he can find."

Rollan nodded. "Fair enough." After Tasha remained stone-faced on the other side of the room, he added, "It was only a suggestion, Tasha. I just want you to be safe."

"The next time you want to volunteer someone to hide from a fight, start with yourself first," Tasha said.

Rollan sighed as Tasha yanked open the door and marched out of the room. "And I thought Meilin was a handful," he muttered.

"Come, my friend," Abeke said. She flexed her arm, and Uraza disappeared. "Let's get breakfast."

Abeke only had a few moments to swallow down her food before she had to rush to gather Kirat and Cabaro's meals. As their primary server, she was solely responsible for delivering breakfast and lunch to Kirat's personal dining room. She quickly loaded the food onto a cart and wheeled it through the halls. She knew she was running late, and prepared herself to be scolded by Kirat and whomever else was in attendance. The bell in the northern tower chimed just as she arrived at the room.

It was empty.

Surely Kirat hadn't left before breakfast. If he had, Sealy would have stopped her from delivering the food. She went ahead and laid all the plates out on the table. She even served the three plates of raw boar for Cabaro.

Finally, Abeke exited the room and slipped down the hallway. She knew where Kirat's personal quarters were located. Perhaps he was still there, preparing for the hunt. She wondered if a boy as spoiled as Kirat even knew how to use a bow and arrow. Or was he only used to being served his food on his father's golden platters?

She arrived to find the door to his quarters slightly ajar. She nudged it open and peered inside. Kirat stood with his back to her, and his arm outstretched. Cabaro was sprawled on the floor in front of him.

"Come on, you stupid lion!" Kirat yelled. "I command you to enter your dormant state."

Cabaro didn't move.

"You can't keep embarrassing me like this. My father will not allow it." He rubbed his arm. "I should just starve you. Maybe then you'll learn your place."

Cabaro let out a loud yawn, then rolled onto his back.

Kirat picked up a pillow from his bed and hurled it at the animal. "You stupid–"

The boy stopped talking as Cabaro growled and leaped to his feet. The lion pinned the pillow between his golden paws and mouth, and ripped it in half with one long, slow pull. He growled again and took a step closer to Kirat. The boy stumbled backward, then quickly climbed onto the bed.

Abeke burst into the room. "Are you okay?"

"Who is–oh, it's only you," Kirat said. He held another pillow between himself and Cabaro–not that it would do any good if the lion really wanted to reach the boy. But Cabaro had already stopped his advance. The lion slowly moved toward a large blanket by the fireplace. He lay down and began grooming himself, looking at Abeke all the while.

"How do you do that?" Kirat asked. His voice was shrill, but he seemed to be genuinely curious. "Why does he respect you, and not me? I am his master."

Abeke moved farther into the room. Perhaps now was the chance to get Kirat on her side. "From what I understand, the bond between humans and spirit animals doesn't work like that. It's a partnership. One does not control the other."

"But my father says–"

"You're the one who has called a spirit animal. Not your father," Abeke said. She paused, letting her words sink in. "How can he guide you on how to work with a spirit animal when he doesn't have one himself?"

Kirat slipped off the bed. Tall and lean, he looked to be a bit younger than her and Rollan. Now that Ninani's Nectar was not required for a stable bond, children as young as eleven had been calling spirit animals all on their own.

"It's comical," he said. "I'm surrounded by the smartest, richest people in Erdas, and the only person I can talk to is someone like you."

Abeke willed herself to hold her temper. Part of her wanted Cabaro to sink his teeth into the boy's flesh. Maybe that would teach *him* to learn his place.

"Perhaps you should try talking to your mother about this," Abeke said. "The other servants say that she's very wise."

"If it was up to her, she would have shipped me off to the Greencloaks as soon as Cabaro appeared."

Abeke's heart leaped. "Yes, the Greencloaks." She thought about her words carefully. She may not have another chance to talk to him. "I've heard that they are the best at helping the newly Marked in their relationships with their spirit animals." She took a step forward. Cabaro shifted but didn't move from his blanket. "I know of a Greencloak in the village. He could take you to their fortress in Greenhaven."

"My father would never let me go. He hates the Greencloaks. They meddle too much in his affairs. Slow down his business. They think they're above the laws of the land."

So does Faisel, Abeke thought. She took a deep breath. "Kirat, you just called Cabaro, one of the mightiest of the Great Beasts," she said. "At some point, you must follow your own heart."

"Perhaps I'll consider it later, after the festival." He pulled a beige linen vest over his silk shirt. "But now, I need to eat. I have to go hunting, even if that stupid animal refuses to enter his dormant state."

Abeke stepped in front of him, stopping him from reaching the door. "I don't think you should wait." She took another deep breath. She knew she was taking a risk but felt she had no choice. "You called Cabaro a few weeks ago, correct? It was a strong connection at first. But then something happened. Something that loosened the connection between you both."

Kirat watched her suspiciously. "It happened two days after I summoned him," he said. "It was like my skin was ablaze. Every joint in my body locked up—I couldn't move, couldn't speak, couldn't think." He frowned. "My father told me to stop complaining. He said that it was part of the process of bonding with Cabaro."

"Your father cannot speak about what he doesn't understand," Abeke said. "What you felt were the effects of a great sickness afflicting the Evertree. It's dying. And once it perishes, so will the bond between humans and spirit animals."

Kirat blinked at her. "How do you know all of this?"

Abeke pushed up her sleeve, showing the mark.

"You have a spirit animal?"

Instead of replying, Abeke released Uraza beside her. The leopard quickly surveyed the room with her violet eyes, before her gaze landed on Cabaro. He had already risen to his feet, and began circling the room.

Clearly, there was no love lost between these two.

"I am Abeke." She patted Uraza. "And as I'm sure you already know, this is Uraza, the Great Leopard."

Kirat's gaze moved from Abeke to Uraza. "You're a Greencloak," he sneered.

"I'm not here to bring you or your family any harm," she said. "But there's a man who is coming to take Cabaro from you. His name is Zerif. He's already stolen most of the Great Beasts from their rightful partners. He won't stop until he's collected them all." She placed her hand on his elbow. "But if you come with me—"

Kirat flung her hand away. "Get off me," he said, his voice rising. Cabaro's growl had grown as well.

"Please, remain calm," Abeke said. "You'll only agitate Cabaro. You have to remember that the connection works both—"

"My father warned me that you all would try to steal me away," he said. "You were one of the Greencloaks who attacked my father's silk shop."

"It wasn't like that. We had to defend ourselves."

Kirat tried to get past Abeke. "Guards! Help!" he yelled. "I'm being kidnapped!"

Abeke had no choice. She punched Kirat in the stomach, causing him to double over. As he fell to the ground, Abeke pulled her dagger from her boot. "Be quiet," she hissed as she pressed the blade to Kirat's throat. "All I want to do is talk."

She glanced at Uraza. She and Cabaro were still staring each other down, but neither had engaged in battle. "Do you see your spirit animal?" she asked Kirat. "Do you understand why he isn't fighting us? We are not your enemy. We're only trying to—"

"What is it?" someone yelled. Abeke froze as two guards entered. "It's another spirit animal!" the other guard yelled. "Get her!"

So much for this plan, Abeke thought as the guards moved toward them. Abeke knew she and Uraza could take them—they were slowed by heavy chain mail. But she also knew that more guards would arrive soon.

As Uraza leaped on one, Abeke ducked as the other swung a curved sword toward her. She kicked her opponent in the leg, then pushed him into the wall. Uraza had the other guard's back against the fireplace.

More footsteps echoed from the hall outside. Abeke turned to Kirat. "You have to come with us. Now!" she yelled.

Kirat shook his head. "I'm not going anywhere with you, Greencloak."

"You're making a terrible mistake," she said. "If Erdas falls, it will be on your conscience." She ran to the door and peeked out. Abeke quickly counted at least five guards sprinting toward Kirat's room. She slammed the door shut and bolted it.

"That's the only way out," Kirat said. "You're trapped." He started toward her, his hands raised as if he wanted to fight.

Abeke picked up a small wooden stool from his vanity and brought it over her head. "Be still," she warned.

Kirat paused but kept his hands balled into fists. Cabaro backed away from Uraza and stood behind Kirat. "You can't escape," Kirat said. "The guards will eventually break down my door."

Abeke looked at the nearest of the room's stained-glass windows. "Then I'll have to find a new way out."

She hurled the stool at the window. The glass shattered everywhere, causing multicolored shards to rain across the carpeted floor and down into the courtyard below.

"No! Stop!" Kirat yelled.

"Stay back," Abeke said, looking at his bare feet. "As pigheaded as you are, I still don't want you to get hurt."

Using one of his satin pillows, she pushed her way through the remaining glass to the now-open window. Abeke ignored the people pointing at her from below, assessing her situation. They were three stories up. Much too high to jump, even with Uraza's help. But just below and to the right of her was another stained-glass window with a ledge. And then another a little below that.

She climbed onto the window frame. "Let's go, Uraza."

Uraza rushed beside her. Cabaro began to follow, but stopped once he noticed that Kirat was not following.

"Kirat, one day you will learn to trust your spirit animal," Abeke said. "I only hope this lesson comes before Zerif steals him from you."

Not waiting for a reply, she stepped out of the window and onto the narrow ledge. "Uraza, give me strength," she murmured. Then she leaped to the next ledge. She let her legs bounce off it, using her inertia to carry her to the one below it, and then to the ground after that.

As soon as Uraza landed behind her, they took off running. There was no point in trying to blend in. Abeke had already drawn too much attention to herself. Many of the guests were wearing their riding gear in anticipation of the large hunt later that morning. They all stopped and stared at her and the dashing leopard, but none of them tried to get in her way. Up above, she heard the sentries yelling, but so far, no arrows came raining down on her and Uraza.

Abeke rushed across the courtyard and burst through another door, and only then did she stop to catch her breath. Although she wasn't as familiar with this part of the fortress, she knew her sleeping quarters were close by. She had to find Rollan and Tasha and warn them. It was only a matter of time before the guards connected her to them.

She crept down a few silent hallways, and slowly, pieces of art began to look familiar. She was close. She had to be. Glancing behind her, she turned the corner and entered the hallway that she believed would finally lead her to Rollan and Tasha.

Then she froze. A sea of arrows was pointed directly at her.

"You're full of surprises," Faisel said as he stood behind the wall of guards. "Unlike my son, I'm sure you've mastered the art of calling your spirit animal into its dormant state."

Abeke swallowed hard. Heat flashed underneath her skin as Uraza returned to the black tattoo on her arm.

"Good girl." Faisel snapped his fingers, and one of the men stepped forward. "Throw her in the dungeon."

13

ON THE RUN

Aᶠᵗᵉʳ ᵇʳᵉᵃᵏᶠᵃˢᵗ, Rollan and Tasha ʳᵉᵗᵘʳⁿᵉᵈ ᵗᵒ their room so they could feed their spirit animals before reporting to serve LaReimaja. Rollan had swiped a few sausage patties and slices of bread while passing though the kitchen. Ninani was already swallowing down the bread, leaving the sausage for Essix. The gyrfalcon had faithfully appeared every morning of her own accord, partially for breakfast, Rollan assumed, and partially to check in. In the past, Rollan could usually call to her with his mind from afar, but he hadn't dared to try since the last bond-breaking incident.

As Rollan stared out the window, waiting for Essix, Tasha began singing again. "Stale bread, stale bread. Eat it hard or go unfed. If you—"

"What is it with you and that song?" Rollan asked.

Tasha shrugged. "It's catchy, don't you think?"

Rollan didn't want to admit it, but it was catchy. And familiar. "Are you sure—"

He was interrupted by a squawk from outside as Essix

swooped down into the window. He offered his arm to her. "Cutting it close, bird."

The falcon shook her head, and took back off.

"What is it?" Tasha asked. "Is Essix not a fan of sausage?"

Rollan dropped the food. "Something's wrong. Essix wants me to see something."

"Do you think it has something to do with Dante?" Tasha asked. "Maybe he took a turn for the worse."

"We'll find out soon enough," Rollan said. He braced himself against the wall. "Lock the door."

Rollan closed his eyes and concentrated.

Nothing.

He squeezed his eyes tighter, and his hands balled into fists. He tried to forget about the smell of sausage and bread in the room. He tried to push aside thoughts of Abeke and Tasha, Meilin and Conor. And then, finally, he saw clouds and blue sky.

Essix was flying fast. Really, really fast. She must have realized that the bond would not remain stable for very long. Essix flew past the harbor and into the market in Caylif. She swooped down toward Faisel's silk shop and landed in an open window.

From what Rollan could tell, most of the damage had been repaired. Essix looked toward the counter in the back of the shop, but a stack of crates blocked her view. The falcon lifted off the windowsill and fluttered farther inside.

Quietly, Essix crept along a bin of multicolored hand-kerchiefs, drawing closer to the back of the shop. She stopped once she had a clear view of the counter. The young boy who had tried to sell to them was there, talking to a man in a hood and dark robe.

Rollan didn't think it was Dante, but he couldn't quite tell. The way the man was turned, he couldn't get a good look at his face.

Suddenly, the man hurled something at the boy's chest. He struggled, then his eyes became blank as a black spiral appeared on his forehead.

The man removed his hood. Zerif.

"Now," Zerif said, handing the boy a knife. "Go get Otto."

The boy disappeared into the back of the store. Otto started yelling a few seconds later. "What are you doing with that—get your hands off me! How dare you!"

The boy dragged Otto to the counter. Zerif didn't bother trying to talk to him. Taking the knife from the boy, Zerif sliced a small incision on Otto's forehead, then pressed a squirming gray parasite to the cut. It buried itself into his skin, then quickly took effect.

"Now take me to Zourtzi," Zerif said. He stopped and sniffed the air. "Actually, wait. I need to take care of something first." He opened his robe, then spun around and looked directly at Essix. A second later, Halawir the Eagle appeared. "Time to add to the collection."

"Essix! Fly!" Rollan yelled. Or maybe he just thought it. He wasn't sure. But the bird didn't need any additional encouragement from Rollan. She had already taken off, though from the sound of it, Halawir was in quick pursuit.

Essix squawked, and then Rollan saw Halawir's large

dark wings and golden beak. Feathers from both birds flashed across Rollan's eyesight.

And then Rollan was falling away, with his vision getting dimmer and dimmer, until he was back in the room at Zourtzi.

"Essix!" he yelled, stretching out his hands as his legs buckled.

Tasha caught Rollan before he completely fell to the floor. She helped him to a bed, then handed him a canteen. "Is something wrong with Essix?" she asked.

Rollan took a few deep breaths, then swallowed a sip of water. His stomach was a jumble of knots, but at least he could still feel the gyrfalcon out there.

"She's okay, I think." *I hope.* He loosed his collar as sweat poured down his neck. "Zerif is in Caylif. He's already infected Otto. He's probably on his way to the castle now." Rollan rose to his feet. Tasha tried to steady him, but he shook his head, and she pulled away. "Abeke was right. Zerif doesn't need an army to scale these walls. Not when he can just get Otto to hand-deliver him to Faisel." He flung the canteen onto his bed. "So much for being impenetrable."

"So now what do we do?"

"We find Abeke, and we talk to LaReimaja. Time to put all our cards on the table." Rollan grabbed two daggers and Tasha picked up a broom.

She leaned it against the wall and stomped on it, breaking the broom's head away from the handle.

"Not quite a staff, but it will have to do."

They opened the door and stepped into the hallway. Suddenly, they heard shouting. "What's going on?" Tasha asked. "Is it an attack? Is it Zerif?"

"It must be something else. Even he can't make it here that quickly." Rollan took off down the hallway, with Tasha close behind. They ran to a window and peered outside. Abeke and Uraza were running full sprint across the courtyard. A garrison of soldiers shouted at her from a few flights above.

"They must have discovered who she was," Tasha said. "We have to help her!"

"Abeke can take care of herself," Rollan said. "We need to find LaReimaja."

"But—"

"Our mission is to get Kirat and Cabaro to safety," he said. "It's what Abeke would want us to do." He watched as Abeke slipped into a large wooden door. "She'll be okay," he said. He didn't really believe that, but he needed Tasha to believe it for now. "We'll be in a better position to help Abeke once we get LaReimaja on our side."

They ran down the hallway toward her quarters. Halfway there, they encountered their first set of guards.

"They're the ones with the Niloan girl!" one of the guards yelled. "Greencloaks! Capture them!"

"Okay, new plan," Rollan said. "We fight our way into her room."

The guard on the left swung his sword. Rollan easily blocked the blow with a dagger, then slashed at him. The blade brushed against the guard's chain mail, doing no real damage. The guard swung again, but Rollan dropped to the ground and put a deep cut into the guard's leg. The man yelled out and fumbled his sword.

Rollan turned to help Tasha, only to see her spinning

through the air, the broom handle twisting in her hands. She clocked the other guard over the head, then landed softly on her feet.

A few steps away, Ninani squawked and flapped her large white wings.

"You know, you should always keep Ninani out," Rollan said as they continued running.

They reached the corridor leading to LaReimaja's quarters, only to find more guards standing in front of her door.

Rollan spun around and began to dash off in the other direction. He quickly skidded to a stop. Three additional guards advanced toward them. And these were not normal guards. They were each accompanied by a spirit animal.

It was the men who had attacked them at the silk shop.

"That's enough, knife-boy," one of the guards finally said as he leveled a crossbow at Ninani's chest. "Not unless you want me to put an arrow through that fancy bird."

Rollan dropped his knife. "Call Ninani into passive form," he said quietly.

The swan raised her wings, then disappeared with a flash of warm radiance.

"I'll alert Lord Faisel," one of the guards said. The others grabbed hold of Rollan and Tasha, walking them back down the hall toward the larger group.

"I can't believe you Greencloak scum thought you could sneak into Zourtzi," one of the guards said. He wore a series of red stripes on his shoulder. He must have been the one in charge. "If you're lucky, Lord Faisel will kill you quickly. Otherwise, he may leave you to starve to death in his dungeon."

Banging sounded from the other side of LaReimaja's door. "What's going on out there?" she yelled. "I demand that you open this door."

"My lady, it isn't safe," the head guard said.

"That is for me to decide," she replied. After a few seconds of silence, she continued. "Tyrus, open this door now. Unless you want to explain to Faisel how you and the men under your command have been taking an extra percentage of my husband's silk profits for yourselves."

Tyrus's tanned face suddenly turned pale. He motioned for the guards to open the door.

LaReimaja stepped out of the room. Her eyes widened as she saw Rollan and Tasha. "What are you doing with those children?"

"They tried to kidnap your son," Tyrus said. "They are not servants. They're Greencloaks in disguise."

LaReimaja's brow furrowed. "Is this true? You're Greencloaks?"

"Yes, but we weren't trying to steal Kirat away," Rollan said. "We only came to warn him about—"

"That's not what Kirat says." Faisel walked up the corridor, flanked by two guards. "He said that your companion attacked him."

"She was only trying to warn him about Zerif," Rollan said.

The guard holding Rollan shook him so hard that his teeth rattled. "Watch your mouth. You are only to speak if Lord Faisel asks you a question."

LaReimaja kept her eyes on Rollan as she walked to her husband. "Is there any truth in what they say?"

"Of course not," he said.

"I know you don't approve of Greencloaks, but perhaps we should listen to them. If our son is really in danger–"

"LaReimaja, watch your tone," Faisel warned. "Remember your place. Your allegiance is to this family now. Not anyone you left behind in Caylif."

And suddenly, Rollan knew.

He was actually surprised it took him so long to piece it all together. There were the carpets and the song that Tasha had been singing. There was LaReimaja's dark hair and tan skin. Her broad shoulders and strong eyes.

"Hey, not all of us Greencloaks are that bad," Rollan said.

Faisel sighed. "Tyrus, please teach our young prisoner some manners."

The head guard grabbed Rollan by the shoulders, then slammed him into the brick wall. "Now shut up."

Rollan's head spun and his eyes watered. "Hey . . . I bet it's pretty dark in your . . . dungeon," he said between spurts of breath. "Can you guys at least spare a torch or a candle?"

Tyrus punched him in the stomach. "Stupid Greencloak. You're begging me to crack your skull."

Rollan coughed and spit up part of his horrible breakfast. Then he took a deep breath and righted himself.

"What do you call a light in your native language?" Rollan asked. He bypassed Tasha's face, her eyes wide and worried, and looked directly at LaReimaja. "Maybe . . . *Lumeo*?"

The guard shook his head as he cocked his arm.

Rollan braced himself as Tyrus's fist came racing toward his face.

Then came the pain.

And then, nothing.

SEA EELS

Surely, Rollan and Abeke must be in a better situation than we are, Meilin thought. In the hours since they had first barricaded themselves in the room, the shouting from beyond the door had stopped. Every so often, Teutar or one of the other pirates would yell at them, reminding them that they couldn't remain in the room forever.

As much as Meilin didn't want to admit it, the pirates were right. Even with the leftover food in the room, she and Takoda would only be able to last a few more days without water. Conor didn't have nearly as long. The parasite was easily visible on his neck now, and steadily moving toward his head.

What will happen to him when the parasite finally takes hold? What happens to Takoda and me if we're stuck in this room with him?

"Has Kovo had enough to eat?" Meilin whispered to Takoda. He made a sign toward Kovo, bunching his fingers together and pressing them against each other. The Great Beast shook his head.

"He's fine," Takoda said.

"Good. So is Jhi, and Briggan, too, I think." The wolf hadn't touched the mushrooms that Conor had tried to feed him but had happily laid into a pile of the fish. "We'll need all of our strength to fight off those pirates." If they could make it to the skiff, they had a chance.

"So how much longer should we wait?" Takoda asked. He readjusted his hold on the sword. Meilin had tried to show him a few pointers—how to parry and block. With Kovo's help, he could probably hold his own against a few of the pirates. She hoped.

Before Meilin could reply, Conor sat down across from her. He'd spent most of his time in the corner, with Briggan and Jhi. But eventually, Jhi had stopped caring for him and returned to the tattoo on Meilin's hand. The panda had done all she could for now.

"Are you ready?" she asked Conor, staring into his blue eyes. Her friend was still there.

He let out a long sigh. "Meilin . . ."

"No," she said. Her voice sounded weaker than she wanted it to be. "Don't you dare even say it."

Conor placed his hand on Meilin's arm. Each of his fingertips sported hard callouses. Such tough hands didn't match his soft, kind face. Had his years of carrying a crook as a shepherd hardened his fingertips, or was it the ax that he had carried into all of their battles together?

"You have a duty. Not to me, but to Erdas," he said. "Let me turn myself over. You and Takoda still have a chance to stop the Wyrm."

Meilin shook her head. "But I can't—"

"Take care of Briggan for me," he said. "Just promise me that."

Meilin offered him a small, quick nod. He rose from the floor and returned to Briggan. As he whispered something to the wolf, Briggan began to whimper.

Kovo grunted, causing both Meilin and Takoda to turn to him. The ape lifted his open hands and then closed them into fists.

"Yes," Takoda said, repeating the gesture. Tears were streaming down the boy's face, but he didn't bother to wipe them away. "He is very brave." Takoda dropped his hands into his lap. "How do you ever become used to this, Meilin? To losing so many people?"

Meilin squeezed her quarterstaff. "You don't," she finally said. "It hurts, every time." She could feel tears forming in her eyes, and she willed them to stay in place. Crying wouldn't do them any good.

She rose to her feet, and Takoda did as well. She cleared her throat as she walked to the door. "We've decided to surrender," she yelled.

"How can we trust you?" someone responded. Meilin thought it was Teutar, but she wasn't sure.

"We'll call back our spirit animals," Meilin said. Then, after looking at Briggan, she added, "All except the wolf. He must remain free."

A few seconds of silence passed. "Come out. Slowly," Teutar finally said.

Kovo pulled back the table, then disappeared onto Takoda's neck. Meilin pulled open the door. At least twenty pirates stood outside of the mess, each carrying a weapon.

Meilin stepped out, followed by Takoda and Conor. Briggan followed, his tail between his legs, head lowered.

Teutar slipped a pair of shackles around Meilin's wrists, while another pirate did the same with Takoda. A third pirate held the pair of shackles meant for Conor, but she seemed too afraid to approach him.

Conor jutted his hands toward her. "Go ahead," he said. "I'm harmless."

"Hurry and do it," Atalanta said as she made her way through the group of pirates. Her gigantic bullfrog was still out, hopping along beside her. Briggan growled but remained in place.

"And someone put a muzzle on that beast," Atalanta added. She stopped in front of Meilin and Takoda. "I should throw you overboard, but what profit would there be in that?"

"Please, you must take us to the Evertree," Meilin said. More like begged. But at this point, her pride was nothing but a distant memory. "You have a spirit animal, just as we do. You must have felt your connection weaken. The bonds will only worsen, and then they will eventually break completely. But we still have time to stop it . . . if you take us to the Evertree."

"I can't take you there. Not even if I wanted to." Atalanta began to pace the deck. "We have noticed all these changes to our land—and not just the Many and the loosening of my bonds with Perth. The sea is different. More dangerous. Creatures that are usually docile and passive are now openly aggressive." She looked out across the water. "The Sulfur Sea is like a moat surrounding the Evertree. The sea itself is usually enough to deter most from trying to reach it. But now there are two large eels guarding the island."

"Xanthe, our guide, told us of three levels of protection," Takoda said. "Could these creatures be part of that?"

Atalanta shook her head. "The wards of protection are meant to stop evil. Those eels have destroyed anything in their path—good and evil alike." She nodded toward Conor. "We can't be sure, but we think they carry the mark of the Many."

"It would be a fool's errand to even attempt to approach the island," Teutar stated. "Those creatures have destroyed ships twice the size of the *Meleager.*"

"You must let us try," Meilin said. "Just give us a boat and point us in the right direction."

"You would be destroyed," Atalanta said.

"We're willing to take that chance," Takoda said.

Atalanta let out a long sigh. "You all are very brave, I'll give you that much." She motioned to one of the pirates. "Ready a set of provisions. Food, water, weapons. Whatever we can spare."

Teutar frowned. "Captain, are you seriously considering their request?" she asked. "Why should we give up our hard-earned food and weapons for a suicide mission? There's no profit in this."

"Teutar, did you not see the animal with them? It was the Great Ape warrior. The one that warned of the Wyrm many eons ago."

"That's impossible," Teutar replied. "That's just a story."

142

"Most stories, however fantastical, hold some version of the truth." Atalanta looked at Takoda. "It *is* him, isn't it?"

"His name is Kovo," Takoda said. "He's one of the Great Beasts of Erdas."

Atalanta turned to Teutar again. "We won't go with them," she said. "But if they can truly stop the Wyrm, then we must allow them to continue." She smiled. "What use is profit at the end of the world?"

Teutar scowled but nodded. "And what of the infected one?"

Atalanta drew her sword. "There's only one choice, I'm afraid."

Meilin stepped to block Atalanta's path. "Please, I beg you. Don't do this. If we stop the Wyrm, we can save him."

"If we don't kill him now, he will infect us all." She nodded to a member of her crew, who picked up Meilin and pulled her out of the way.

Briggan whimpered again. "No, it's okay," Conor said softly. His blue eyes were crystal clear and free of tears. "It's okay . . ."

Then, suddenly, he began to convulse. Teutar pulled her sword from its sheath. "He's changing! We must kill him now, before he fully converts."

"No!" Meilin said. "The parasite is still at his neck. It's something else!"

Conor's body shook so hard that Meilin was afraid his neck was going to snap. Finally, he settled, pointing a shaky finger out to the sea. "It's coming."

Just then, a horn blared from the crow's nest—one long blow, followed by two short ones in rapid succession.

"There's something out there," Teutar said. "Something fast."

Atalanta snapped her fingers, and a second later someone had placed a telescoping spyglass into her hand. She extended it and looked out to the sea. She inhaled sharply. "Battle stations!"

"What about them?" Teutar asked, nodding toward Meilin and the others.

"Release them," Atalanta commanded. "We'll need all the help we can get."

The pirates removed their shackles, then began to scramble. Some grabbed crossbows and arrows while others began to load the cannons.

"What is it?" Meilin asked Conor. "What's coming?"

"I . . . I don't know," Conor said. "But it's big."

Meilin looked back toward the sea. She could see ripples in the mustard-colored water as something below the surface raced toward them. Another horn sounded, and the first volley of cannonballs fired. Whatever was in the water didn't seem at all bothered by the firepower.

"Reload," one of the pirates yelled.

"Too late!" another screamed.

A pair of large, scaly eels breeched the surface of the water. Their snouts bore the huge black swirling marks of the parasite.

In a way, the eels reminded Meilin of the dragon kites flown in Zhong's New Year Festival. But these creatures were nothing like a child's toy. They let out screeching yells, each showing off a pair of curved, sharp fangs and long, forked tongues. Yellow water dripped down their shiny skin as they arched their bodies. Glaring down on the ship, the eels seemed to focus their dark red eyes right at Meilin and Conor.

The eels let out more earsplitting screeches as they slammed their bodies into the sea, creating a tidal wave. The *Meleager* groaned as it tipped on its port side. Crates and containers snapped loose from their tie-downs and slid across the polished deck. Meilin leaped into Conor, pushing him out of the way just before a rolling cannonball collided with his legs.

He blinked, and it took a few seconds for his eyes to land on Meilin. "Oh, thanks," he said.

"Conor, you have to focus!" Meilin said. She pointed toward a few pirates desperately holding on to the railing. "You and Takoda pull them back up," Meilin said. "Then help with loading the cannons. I'm going to find Atalanta."

Takoda called forth Kovo. He, Conor, and their spirit animals all raced toward the pirates hanging on to the railing, while Meilin ran toward the ship's bow. There stood Atalanta and Teutar, their arms wrapped around the railing.

"Ready those cannons!" Atalanta barked as Meilin reached them. "One of the eels is coming back around."

"But where's the other one?" Teutar asked. "It must be—"

"There!" Meilin yelled, pointing to a long, muddy shadow curving toward the boat. "It's about to hit us!"

Meilin had just enough time to brace herself against the rail before the eel rammed into the ship. Meilin flew forward, badly skinning her knee and arms, while Atalanta, Teutar, and Atalanta's bullfrog slammed into the deck. Planks of wood splintered and cracked all around them, and one of the ship's large masts snapped off and fell into the sea.

Meilin pulled herself up and crawled to Atalanta. She was huddled over her bullfrog.

"Is he all right?" Meilin asked.

"Perth will be fine," she said. "Unfortunately, I cannot say the same for the *Meleager*. We're already taking on water."

"What can we do to help?" Meilin asked.

"Can you serve as runners from the armory to the cannons?" Teutar asked. A trail of blood dripped from a cut on her forehead. "Half of our gunpowder just went overboard."

"No," Atalanta said. "Go to the armory but forget the powder. Grab whatever weapons you need and get off this ship." Then she turned to Teutar. "Swing us around and open the sails. We're going to the Evertree."

"But we don't stand a chance—"

"Girl, do as I say!" the captain yelled as her skin exploded in blue light. "The *Meleager* is already lost. We don't stand a chance against those eels. If we can get them to the Evertree, perhaps they can save Sadre before—"

Another eel rammed into the ship.

Atalanta, Meilin, and Teutar fell to the deck.

Perth, Atalanta's bullfrog, went overboard.

"No!" Atalanta yelled. She reached futilely for the space where the bullfrog had just been. She rose to her feet and peered over the edge. "I can't see him, but I can feel him. He's alive."

"Can you call him back?" Meilin asked.

Atalanta shook her head, frantically scanning the water. "He's too far away. The bonds are too weak." She began unbuttoning her jacket.

"No, Atalanta!" Teutar said, grabbing her arm. "You can't."

Atalanta gave her a sad smile. "My child, he is my spirit animal. I have to try. I would sooner lose my legs than lose him."

"But the water . . . the eels," Teutar stammered. "You'll drown."

"Better to die a hero than live a coward." She removed her jacket and flung it aside. "Take care of the crew, Teutar. They're your burden now. And when you tell my story, make sure it's a good one."

With that, Atalanta pulled her sword from its scabbard and leaped over the railing.

Meilin and Teutar watched silently as Atalanta dove into the water. They waited and waited.

She never resurfaced.

"I'm sorry," Meilin said.

Meilin's voice seemed to awaken the ship's new captain. "Why are you still standing here?" Teutar demanded through clenched teeth. She shoved Meilin away from her. "Go downstairs and gather your provisions." Then Teutar cupped her hands over her mouth and yelled to the pirate steering the ship. "Open the sails and turn her around! We sail to the Evertree!"

Teutar took a flight of stairs to the bridge of the ship

and began helping to spin the wheel. Meilin cast one last glance over the railing. There was still no sign of Atalanta. Teutar was the new captain of the ship.

Meilin took the stairs to the armory below and grabbed as many weapons as she could find—swords, knives, and a quarterstaff. She even found a few glowstones. She felt the ship swinging around and tried to keep her balance as the eels continued to pummel the hull.

By the time she made it back upstairs, she could tell that the ship was riding dangerously low in the water. She found Takoda and the others at a cannon, firing round after round at the eels that ran along the ship's bow. The *Meleager* was slicing though the water, but the eels were just as fast.

"Come on," she said. "We've got to go!"

"But what about the cannons?" Takoda asked.

"It's pointless," she said. "We have to abandon ship."

She led the others back to Teutar. The woman stood alone at the ship's wheel, struggling to keep the *Meleager* on course, despite blow after blow from the eels. Finally, she let go—just as the wheel began to spin uncontrollably. "The rudder broke off. I can no longer steer."

"How close are we to the Evertree?" Meilin asked.

"As close as you're going to get," Teutar said. She raced from the bridge to one of the skiffs. It was attached to a large wooden crane meant to safely lower the boat into the water. "Aim that way," she said, pointing a shaky finger out into the darkness. "The current will guide you there."

"Come with us," Meilin said. "The ship can't take much more damage."

For the first time since meeting her, Teutar smiled. "I am the captain. I cannot abandon my crew. Now get on board. I'll lower you down."

Meilin climbed aboard first, followed by the others. Kovo remained on deck. "What's wrong with him?" Meilin asked Takoda. "Whether he likes it or not, he's got to come with us."

"It's not that," Takoda said as Kovo gently nudged Teutar out of the way. Then the large ape rose up and pushed the boat so it was dangling over the water.

Takoda leaned over the side of the boat. "Thank you, Teutar."

"Good luck," she replied. Then she nodded to Kovo. He let out a booming roar, then smashed the wooden crane holding the lifeboat to the ship.

Meilin's stomach instantly flew into her mouth as they plummeted straight down. The fall seemed to take hours. Finally, they crashed into the sea with an impact that sent Meilin's teeth rattling. A second later, something large splashed into the water beside them.

"It's Kovo!" Conor yelled. "Pull him in."

"I have a better idea." Takoda closed his eyes, and Kovo disappeared from the water, materializing as a tattoo on the boy's neck. Then, as fast as he was gone, he reappeared inside the boat.

"Row!" Meilin said. "We have to get as far away from the ship as we can. We can't let their sacrifice be in vain."

Everyone picked up an oar and started rowing furiously. Meilin's hands, arms, and back screamed in pain, but she continued to paddle. Every few minutes, she cast a look back at the *Meleager* as it sank farther and farther into the sea. The boom of the ship's cannons still rang in her ears long after they had stopped firing.

They kept rowing. And the *Meleager* kept sinking.

She thought about asking Conor if he could see any ships in the water. Any survivors. But she chose not to. She didn't want to know the answer.

Finally, a stretch of shore appeared ahead.

"Aim for the small inlet to the left," Meilin said. "We have to get out of the water before the eels come."

They redoubled their efforts. Meilin put every ounce of power, anger, and fear into each stroke.

Once they reached the shore, they grabbed the packs Meilin had scavenged from the *Meleager* and stumbled out of the boat. Something large and dark loomed before them, but it was too difficult to see without any light. Meilin tried to open her pack, but her fingers had cramped up too much for her to work the latch.

"Massage your fingers first," Takoda said, kneeling beside her in the sand. "If you're not careful, you could do some real damage." He reached out to her. "Here, let me help rub your hands."

Meilin shook her head. "In a second. First, can you light a glowstone? We need to see where we are. Something's up ahead, but I can't tell what it is."

Takoda nodded, then took the pack from her. After he found the glowstone, he struck it and held it up for them to see.

The outline of a ruined city stretched before them.

"It's . . . huge," Conor said. His voice was shaking. "I bet it's even bigger than Phos Astos."

Kovo grunted and pointed above. They all looked up to see the silver roots of the Evertree stretching out across the top of the cavern.

And there—high above the city and nestled in the Evertree's roots—was a black, oozing polyp. It looked like a rotted egg, with a giant crack in its side.

Meilin took a deep breath. "The Wyrm."

15

THE ATTACK

ABEKE'S CELL WAS DARK AND COLD. IT WAS ONE OF MANY in Zourtzi's dungeon, but Abeke believed she was alone. She hadn't heard any voices coming from the other cells, at least. She only recognized the sounds of rodents scurrying around the dungeon. Perhaps she should release Uraza, she thought. The leopard could use a snack.

As she sat there, Abeke found herself thinking about the last time she had been imprisoned. Shane, her friend—*former* friend—had been her captor. At the time, Abeke hadn't known that he was the Devourer. The King of Stetriol. He'd passed himself off as a helpless pawn in the war between the Conquerors and the Greencloaks, even while keeping her in chains in the brig of a ship, and later, the dungeon of a Niloan manor not so different from this one.

Even when Meilin had warned Abeke about trusting him, Abeke had chosen to put her faith in Shane. He was her friend. He cared for her. And it looked like her friendship would be rewarded, as Shane helped her to escape and returned with her to Greenhaven. She discovered too late that it was only a ruse, so he could sneak into the Greencloak stronghold and betray them from within.

Now she wondered if her instincts had failed her again. She knew she had pushed Kirat—perhaps too fast—but she had no other choice. She could only hope that Rollan and Tasha had been able to escape.

She leaped to her feet as the heavy door to the dungeon swung open. Then, just as quickly, her heart sank. Tasha was led in first, a guard on each side of her. Abeke gasped. The guards were dragging Rollan in. He was unconscious. Or worse.

The main guard unlocked the heavy iron gate to Abeke's cell. They shoved Tasha in, pushing her into Abeke. Then they brought Rollan inside. They glanced around the bare cell, perhaps searching for something to lay him on. The cold stone floor was barely covered with hay.

Abeke struggled to her feet. "Please don't drop him," she managed to say, rushing forward. She froze as one of the guards aimed an arrow at her. She held up her hands. "I just want to help my friend."

"Give him to her," the main guard said. "Lord Faisel will want to interrogate him later. The boy can't talk if his head is splattered all across the floor."

Holding Rollan in her arms, Abeke half-dragged, half-carried him to the corner. Tasha had already begun collecting as much straw as possible to create something soft to rest his head on. Abeke laid him down and inspected him. Blood ran from his nose, and a spot on his forehead had already turned purple.

"What happened to Rollan?" Abeke asked as the guard locked the cell and left the dungeon.

Tasha ripped a piece of cloth from her skirt and started to clean Rollan's face. "He wouldn't shut up. He kept talking, even when the guards warned him to stop." She shook her head. "I have no idea why."

Abeke patted her friend's hand. "I'm so sorry," she said. She wanted to talk to him, even though she wasn't sure if he could hear her. "If I hadn't pushed Kirat about leaving, none of this would have happened." She took the cloth from Tasha and took over cleaning the dried blood from his face. "For a moment, I thought I had convinced him. Even Cabaro seemed to be on our side. Then he summoned the guards. I thought I would be able to escape, but the guards eventually surrounded me."

Tasha moved closer to Abeke. "Do you have any ideas on how we can get out of here?" she whispered. "Maybe we could somehow get to that window," she said, pointing up.

"There's no way we could climb that high," Abeke said, touching the cell's walls. "But perhaps, once Rollan wakes up, he and I can boost you up there."

"I'm not leaving without you," Tasha said forcefully. "If we can't get out through the window, then—as Rollan would say—we'll have to come up with a new plan. We'll fight our way out."

Tasha's braid had come undone, and wispy strands of white-blond hair lay plastered to her forehead. The girl's eyes seemed harder than before. Tasha had grown up so much since meeting Abeke and Rollan. What happened to the shy, awkward girl who had loved reading books? Abeke wondered. Would she ever return?

"We can discuss this when Rollan wakes up," Abeke finally responded. "And perhaps Rollan was right. Maybe we'll be better off in Zourtzi, even if it's in the dungeon."

"No," Tasha said, her eyes wide. "That's why we were trying to get to LaReimaja. We were trying to warn her. Zerif is in Caylif. Rollan saw him through Essix's eyes. Zerif infected Otto with one of those parasite things."

"Then we don't have much time," Abeke said. She looked back at the window. "As soon as Rollan wakes, we have to get you out of here."

"Like I said—I'm not leaving you two," Tasha repeated. "And don't preach to me about the mission, or protecting Erdas, or anything like that." Tears had welled in her eyes and began spilling down her cheeks. "You and Rollan are the only people I know. The only people I have left in this world. I don't even want to think about what might have happened to my parents—" She stopped talking as a sob escaped from her throat.

"Okay," Abeke said softly. "We'll figure something out." She searched around the cell. "Maybe we can just release our spirit animals. Ninani could fly out the window. And while Uraza won't like swimming from the castle, she could do it if she had to." Abeke turned back to Rollan. "But we'll wait until Rollan wakes before we decide anything."

She squeezed his hand. *Please wake up.*

A churring sound came to the window above. Abeke looked up and smiled as a familiar face appeared. Essix. "He's okay," she said to the Great Beast. "We'll take care of him."

Abeke wasn't sure how much time had passed when she heard talking from outside the dungeon door. She nudged Tasha, who had nodded off. *Get ready*, she mouthed. *Faisel.*

Rollan still hadn't woken up, but Abeke couldn't take the risk of waiting for him. If she and Uraza rushed the guards as soon as they opened the cell, and if Tasha held back to protect Rollan, she figured that they had a chance.

The heavy, thick door swung open. A guard awkwardly entered the dungeon, but instead of heading toward them, he walked toward a nearby cell. No, not walked. Someone was pushing him.

A woman stood behind him, her face covered by a red cloak and hood. *Could it be one of the Redcloaks who helped us before?*

"LaReimaja!" Tasha yelled, jumping to her feet.

The woman smiled as she pushed the tip of her sword into the guard's back. "Ahmar, take his keys."

Ahmar, the servant who had been helping Abeke, entered with a ring of keys in his hand. He unlocked the empty cell and pushed the guard into it. He then bound the guard's mouth closed with a scarf. "We don't have much time, my lady," Ahmar said to LaReimaja once he had finished.

"Where are their bags?" she asked him.

"I sent one of my helpers to collect them."

"I hope it's someone you can trust." She nodded toward Abeke and Tasha. "Unlock the cell."

Ahmar did as he was instructed, and they both entered the cell. Abeke didn't know what to say to the woman. Her son favored her—he had clearly inherited his skin and long frame from her. But there was something else that felt familiar about her.

LaReimaja knelt in front of Rollan. She softly placed her sword on the ground and checked his pulse. "I am sorry," she whispered as she pulled her hood from her head. "But we don't have time for you to wake on your own." She pulled a small pouch from her belt, then poured a pinch of dried multicolored herbs into her tanned hands. Abeke covered her nose—she could smell the stench from all the way across the cell.

"Concentrated ginger and xercia," she said. "If this won't wake him up, nothing will." She pulled Rollan onto her lap, cradling his head, then pressed the herbs to his nostrils. At first, nothing happened. Abeke's heart thundered.

Suddenly, Rollan jerked awake. "What? Who—"

"Calm down, Rollan," LaReimaja said, patting his cheeks. "Take a moment to gather yourself. You took quite a blow to the head."

Tasha stepped forward. "How do you know his name?" she demanded. There was a coldness to her voice, something Abeke hadn't heard from her before. "I know he never told it to you." They had all been together when Rollan reminded Tasha not to reveal her real name, as that could compromise their ruse.

"I don't know who *you* are," LaReimaja said to Tasha.

"But once Faisel mentioned that one of the Greencloaks had Uraza the Leopard as a spirit animal, I knew it had to be Abeke of Nilo." She put her hand against Rollan's forehead. "Which would make him Rollan, caller of Essix the Falcon."

"Her name is Tasha," Rollan said. "She called Ninani the Swan, though with the way my head is pounding, I really wish it had been Jhi. I would kill for a little magical healing right about now."

"I heard you were a jokester," LaReimaja said. "I can see why my brother was so close to you. So close to you all."

Abeke moved forward. "I don't understand. Your brother?"

Rollan grinned. "Abeke, I would like to introduce you to Reima. Tarik's younger sister."

"*Reima*," the woman repeated softly. "I haven't been called that in a very long time. Tarik gave me that nickname."

Abeke stared at the woman. She could see it now, the similarities between her and their former guardian. "How did you know?"

"Well, I didn't for sure," Rollan replied as he sat up. He gingerly touched the bruise on his head. "But there were a lot of little clues, like the carpets, and the song that Tasha overheard Reima singing to force herself to eat bad food . . . and Kirat's name."

"It was two years before Faisel realized that his son's name was Tarik spelled backward," LaReimaja said with a laugh. "He didn't speak to me for a month, but there was little he could do about it at that point."

Essix left her perch at the window and flew into the cell, landing on Rollan's shoulder. "Hey there, girl," Rollan said. "I knew you could handle yourself against Halawir." He opened his shirt, and the falcon disappeared as a tattoo on his skin. "Tarik only mentioned you once, but when he did, it was clear that he cared greatly for you," he said as he refastened his shirt. "Tarik also mentioned that something else had happened—something that he didn't want to talk about, even with me."

The woman gave them a sad smile. "Our family did well for many years after Tarik left us to join the Greencloaks. Then the carpet shop fell on hard times, and my father became gravely ill." She twisted the weathered gold ring on her finger. "Faisel was rich and had always fancied me . . . and my family's business. He proposed our union as more of a merger than a marriage. It would allow me to obtain the expensive medicine that my father desperately needed, and it would strengthen Faisel's carpet business. Of course, it also resulted in a beautiful son. Spoiled, but beautiful." She sighed. "But before I could marry Faisel, I had to denounce all my ties to my brother, because he was a Greencloak." She nodded toward Ahmar, who stood just outside the cell. "Ahmar grew up with me and Tarik. He would pass news my way about my brother whenever he heard rumors in the market. It was Ahmar who told me that the Four Fallen had returned, and that Tarik had been chosen to serve as the guardian of their human partners. I was—am—so proud. It was only recently that I learned of his death." She looked at Rollan. "How did he die?"

Rollan's mouth fell open—maybe the first time that Abeke had seen him without a quick response. She was sure that Rollan was struggling with what to tell her. How would LaReimaja feel knowing that her brother died here in Nilo, partially because of the stubbornness and cowardice of Cabaro, her son's spirit animal?

"He died honorably," Abeke finally said. "A Greencloak to the end."

"He saved my life," Rollan added. "And now, you're doing the same."

Abeke tensed as footsteps echoed down the hallway. Someone was approaching.

"I retrieved their belongings," a servant said, entering the dungeon. She lifted the cover on her tray, revealing Abeke's pack. "But we must hurry. I told the guards at the top of the stairs that I was coming to bring food for the prisoners. I fear that they will become suspicious."

"Then go," LaReimaja said. She took the pack and handed it to Abeke. "We'll find another way to get out."

The servant nodded at LaReimaja before casting a worried look at Ahmar. She disappeared out the door.

Abeke opened the bag and pulled out the few remaining weapons. She threw a green cloak to Tasha before fastening her own around her neck. She then handed Rollan his cloak. She expected him to put it on, but instead he just held it.

Of course. Tarik's cloak.

Abeke motioned for Tasha to follow her out of the cell. "Give him a minute," she whispered.

"What's going on?" Tasha asked.

"It's Rollan's story to tell, not mine."

Abeke watched as Rollan spoke to LaReimaja in hushed tones. He handed her the cloak, and she took it into her arms and breathed it in. Then she slowly returned it to Rollan. He tried to push it back into her hands, but she refused. Then she took a small pendant from her neck, pressed it into Rollan's palm, and whispered something in his ear.

Rollan and LaReimaja joined the others outside the cell. "Rollan says that you have to take my son with you," she said, sliding her sword back in its sheath. "Is this Zerif really that dangerous?"

Tasha nodded. "His forces overthrew the imperial castle of Stetriol in a matter of minutes," she said.

"He's on his way to Zourtzi now," Abeke added. "Taking Kirat away from here is the only way we can protect him and Cabaro."

"And where will you take him? Greenhaven?"

Abeke didn't falter. "We'll take him somewhere safe. Somewhere that Zerif can't reach him."

LaReimaja looked at each of the children before letting her gaze land on Rollan. "So be it." She walked toward the door. "Come. There's a secret staircase built into the west wall. That will give us the best chance of reaching Kirat's quarters unnoticed."

LaReimaja pulled the hood back over her head so that only her chin was exposed. She peeked her head out the door, then stepped into the hallway. Ahmar followed her out next, and then the others.

Once they reached the wall, she pulled back the

green-and-gold tapestry to reveal what seemed to be solid brick. Abeke narrowed her eyes and looked closer—she could faintly see the pattern of a door in the brick.

"We just have to find the lever to open it," LaReimaja whispered. She began pushing on each brick on the wall. "Help me, children. Try the lower ones. Ahmar, you watch our back."

The servant nodded as he readjusted his sweaty hold on a butcher's knife. While LaReimaja seemed so confident and sure of herself, Ahmar looked like he was a few seconds away from dropping his weapon and retreating to the safety of his quarters.

"Be sure to try the ones all the way at the bottom," LaReimaja said. "The lever has to be here somewhere."

They tried every brick they could reach—some two or three times. When that plan didn't work, they tried to push the door itself. It refused to budge.

"Maybe we should turn back and try another way," Abeke said.

LaReimaja shook her head. "There is no other way. The guards' quarters are right off the main staircase. There's no way we can sneak past them."

"Wait. Up there!" Tasha yelled. She pointed all the way to the top. A small brick seemed to jut slightly out of the wall.

"He must trigger it with an arrow," LaReimaja said. "If we throw a knife—"

"I have a better idea," Tasha said. Ninani appeared beside her with a flash. Tasha picked up the swan, nearly toppling under the bird's weight, and pointed to the top of wall. "See it, Ninani?"

The swan nodded. Tasha threw her into the air, and Ninani flapped her wings and soared to the top of the wall. She struck the brick with her beak, and the door immediately receded backward.

"Good job," Tasha said as the swan returned to her.

"We should all call our spirit animals," Abeke said. "Best to be prepared. We won't know what to expect at the top of the stairs."

"I finally get Essix to go passive, and you want me to pull her right back out?" The falcon appeared in the air beside Rollan, her wings spread wide. "Hey, don't look at me," he said to the bird. "It was Abeke's idea."

They entered the stairwell and pushed the door shut behind them. LaReimaja lit one of the torches sitting in a metal sconce on the wall. The air inside the stairwell was stale and hot. Abeke immediately felt claustrophobic.

Ahmar followed LaReimaja up the stairs. "My lady," he mumbled. "How will you get them out?"

"There is a secret exit in Faisel's study," she said.

"I know," he said. "But even then, how will they get across the sea without being noticed?"

"One problem at a time."

"But, my lady—"

"Just say what you're really thinking, Ahmar," LaReimaja said.

He gulped. "Aren't you worried about what Lord Faisel will do once he discovers what you—what *we*—have done?"

She shook her head. "My old friend, thank you for all of your help. You can leave us. I won't hold it against you. And I'll make sure Faisel understands that I forced you to assist me."

His face relaxed. "But, my lady, what about you?"

"The only person I love more than my brothers is my son. I will not let harm come to him, no matter the consequences to me." She continued up the stairs. "Enough talk. Wait until we reach the top, and then return to your room," she said.

Rollan snapped his fingers. "If you don't mind, I'll borrow that knife."

Ahmar handed it to him. "Good luck."

The staircase was long and winding, with uneven steps. They lit what torches they could, but the sconces were spaced very far apart, causing them to pass through some stretches in complete darkness.

They were almost at the top of the staircase when a loud explosion rocked the castle.

"What was that?" Tasha asked, bringing up the rear of the group. "A cannon?"

"Impossible," LaReimaja said as she raced up the last few steps. "There isn't a ship in Erdas that could launch a cannonball into Zourtzi's walls. The waters surrounding us are too shallow for a ship that large."

LaReimaja pushed open the door, causing light to spill into the stairway. "Follow me," she said. "It's empty."

They ran down the hall, pausing momentarily when another cannon shook the fortress. Rollan went to a window and gasped. "Look!"

They crowded around him. Zourtzi was indeed being fired on—by its own cannons. From where they stood, they could see the cannons on two of the towers pointed at the castle's interior walls. Below, some of the fortress's guards shot arrows at the men manning the towers. But whenever one hit, another man would immediately take his place.

"Over there!" Tasha said, pointing.

Outside the castle, a swarm of people swam across the sea. Those closer to the castle, in the shallow part of the channel, were climbing over the man-made reefs. Animals swam and ran alongside them.

They were too far away to see if any of the attackers carried a black swirl on their forehead, but they could easily see the green cloaks around many of their shoulders.

"Are those all the Greencloaks?" Tasha asked. "There are so many."

Abeke forced herself to look away from the swarm of Greencloaks. "It's hard to say. I don't know how many were in Greenhaven." For once, Abeke was glad that Meilin and Conor were trapped underground. She didn't know if she would have been able to fight her friends if they had been the ones storming the fortress.

"How many of the fortress guards have spirit animals?" Abeke asked LaReimaja.

"A handful," LaReimaja replied. "But not enough to stop an army of Greencloaks." She sighed. "Zourtzi will fall. It's inevitable."

"Look alive, guys," Rollan said, turning. "We have company."

A group of ten soldiers came barreling down the hallway, their weapons drawn. But instead of attacking, they stopped in front of the group. "We've been ordered by Lord Faisel to escort you and Kirat to safety," one of them said.

"Good, let's go," LaReimaja said. They continued to Kirat's room. LaReimaja flung the door open, not even bothering to knock.

Kirat stood at his closet, with Cabaro close by him. A bag was in Kirat's hand, half full of clothes.

"Mother!" He ran to her and they embraced. "One of the guards was just here," he said. "We have to leave."

"I know." She took the bag from him and threw it on the floor. "Forget the clothes. Grab whatever weapons you have." She turned to Abeke. "You prefer a bow and arrow, yes? Kirat has a brand-new bow and a quiver full of arrows in that top drawer," she said.

"Mother!" Kirat exclaimed. "What are you doing with these prisoners? Why are you giving her my bow? It was a gift from Father."

"Yes. A gift you never learned to use," she said. "Best to give it to someone who knows what she's doing with it."

Abeke found the bow. As she slung the strap of the quiver over her shoulder, she noticed Uraza and Cabaro circling each other.

"Play nice, Uraza," she said.

Uraza hissed as she walked away from Cabaro. The lion growled at Ninani and Essix. Neither bird moved.

"I think they're used to his empty threats," Rollan said. "No lionesses to fight for you this time, Cabaro?"

The lion snarled at Rollan. He wisely backed up.

"Mother, what's going on?" Kirat asked. "I demand that you tell me what you're doing with these

Greencloaks!" He pointed to Abeke. "Especially that one. You see what she did to my room. My window! If father knew you were—"

"Enough with the questions," LaReimaja snapped. Then she sighed. "My son, you are spoiled. I'm sorry about that, as it's as much my fault as anyone else's. But today you must grow up." She pointed to one of the guards. "You—give me one of your swords." She took it, then pressed it into her son's hands. "I hope you haven't forgotten everything you learned in all those dueling lessons."

Rollan picked up a staff leaning against the wall. "Better than a broomstick, right?" he asked, handing it to Tasha. "Ready?"

She spun the weapon in her hands. "Ready as I'll ever be. And what about you?"

He held a dagger in one hand, and Ahmar's knife in the other. "I'll be fine."

"I'll take the lead," Abeke said as she nocked an arrow into the bow's string. "Can we get to Faisel's study from the secret passage?"

"Yes," LaReimaja said. She turned to the guards. "Kirat, stay close to me. Guards, take up the rear."

The walls had already begun to collapse as they made their way back to the stairway. Uraza walked in front of Abeke, deftly leaping over the huge chandeliers that had fallen from the ceiling and the large marble statues that lay broken in their path. Even with a faint bond, Abeke could feel Uraza's energy coursing through her own body as she sidestepped the bits of debris that continued to fall around them.

Uraza's ears flattened as they reached the door. Abeke could hear it as well. There were voices in the stairway.

She nodded to one of the guards. With his sweat-covered forehead, he reminded her of Ahmar. "Pull it open," she said. "But slowly. I'll look inside."

As he cracked open the door, Abeke raised her bow and peeked down the passageway. A swarm of guards, guests, and Greencloaks quickly climbed up the stairs. Each bore the mark of the parasite on their foreheads. Leading the pack was Ahmar, his face now a blank canvas. Directly behind him was Dante, his arm still covered in a white bandage. Abeke wondered how Zerif had found him.

"What do you see?" one of the guards asked behind her.

Abeke waved her hand behind her, trying to get the guard to remain quiet, but it was too late. The swarm of people had heard them and were now rushing up the stairs.

"Close it!" she yelled. "We need to find another way down."

The guard slammed the door shut, while two others dragged a statue to it. They propped it against the door. "That should stop them," the bearded one said.

Rollan shook his head. "No, it won't."

LaReimaja pointed to three of the guards with the end of her sword. "You three will take Kirat and the Greencloaks to Faisel's study. Don't use the main stairs—try the ones in the southwest corner. That will give you the best chance of making it to the bottom level unnoticed." She looked at her son. "There is a small exit built into the floor underneath your father's desk. Take that tunnel—it will lead you to the outside of the south wall. From there, you will have to find a way to Caylif. But I know you can do it."

Kirat lowered his sword. "But . . . you're not coming with us?" he asked, his voice quiet as realization dawned on his face.

She shook her head. "We will remain to hold them off."

Just then, they heard pounding from the stairwell. The door, braced by the statue, held. For now.

"Mother," Kirat said. Tears had formed in the corners of his eyes.

"Be brave," she said, hugging her son. "Remember, your uncle was a great warrior—his blood flows through your veins, too." She turned to Rollan. "Tarik gave his life for yours. In return, you are now responsible for my son's life. He's in your care."

Rollan nodded and gave her a small bow. "I won't fail you."

They took off down the hallway while LaReimaja and the remaining soldiers readied themselves. Abeke slowed down and glanced behind her once she had reached the top of the stairs at the end of the hallway. LaReimaja had positioned herself and the other guards right in front of the door—probably to try and cut down the infected as they exited. It's exactly what Tarik would have suggested.

Abeke joined the others, who had already started down the staircase. It didn't take Uraza's enhanced hearing to know that there was a battle going on downstairs.

"I'm not sure how much better off we are going this way," Tasha said. "It sounds pretty bad down there."

"Is there another way to Faisel's study?" Abeke asked the bearded guard.

"We could try the main stairs," he replied. "But we would be totally exposed. Anyone fighting in the foyer would see us as soon as we started down." He hesitated. "Maybe we should go back."

"No," Abeke said. "We cannot fight what is up above."

"There are more sentries downstairs," the youngest of the guards answered. "We have a fighting chance." He shrugged. "At least, a better chance than . . ."

He must have noticed the twisted and sad look on Kirat's face. "I'm sorry, my lord."

"Apologize later," Rollan said. "Let's go. We have to make the most of the time LaReimaja bought us."

"Agreed," Abeke said. "We'll try to sneak down and get as close as we can before they notice us. We'll engage whenever we have to."

Abeke and Uraza moved to take the lead. The winding staircase was built like a corridor with high walls. They wouldn't be seen by anyone downstairs until the last turn.

Suddenly, they heard footsteps rushing up the stairs. Abeke steadied her bow, ready to sink her arrow into whomever appeared. Then she gasped as the figure turned the corner.

Olvan!

170

He was riding his moose, which was almost too large for the small staircase. The spiral on Olvan's forehead seemed to swirl with every step closer he came. He growled at them, and his moose matched him with a deep, guttural moan. Abeke was glad that the staircase was so steep and narrow. She was sure that the Greencloak leader would have reached them by now if he had been on foot.

"What are you waiting for?" Kirat asked. "Kill him."

"I . . . I can't." She glanced over her shoulder at Rollan, hoping that he would have a plan. His face had paled, and his mouth hung open.

"What should I do?" Abeke asked him.

Rollan's eyes were glassy as he shook his head. He either couldn't answer, or wouldn't.

Abeke turned back around. Olvan's moose had sped up—he would be within striking distance soon. She raised her bow again and pointed her arrow at the swirl on his forehead. Would she forever be remembered as the girl who killed the great Olvan?

Abeke took a deep breath, shifted her aim, and released the arrow. It sank into Olvan's shoulder, causing him to fall off his moose. He tumbled backward down the stairs, before landing awkwardly on his arm. The moose, suddenly free of Olvan, reared back, then charged them.

Uraza sprang forward, landing right in front of the beast. She lowered herself to the ground, a deep growl in her throat. The moose lunged and tried to swipe her with his antlers, but Uraza slipped to the side and ran her claws against his flank. The moose swung again, this time catching Uraza and slamming her against the wall. She seemed dazed, but she quickly rose to her feet and took a defensive stance against the animal.

"Watch out for his hooves," Abeke said as the moose began to stomp. She tried to aim her arrow at the creature but was afraid that she would miss and hit Uraza instead.

"Kirat, ask Cabaro to help," Rollan said. "If he and Uraza work together, they can stop Olvan's moose."

Kirat shook his head. "Why should I put my animal in danger? We wouldn't be in this mess if she had shot him like I demanded."

"For crying out loud, get over yourself!" Tasha said. "If you and Cabaro are too scared to fight, Ninani and I will do so in your place. Ready, Ninani?"

But Ninani wasn't preparing to join the battle. Instead, she was standing in front of Cabaro, staring at him. The lion tried to move out of the way, but Ninani kept placing herself in front of him, her eyes boring into the lion's. Finally, Cabaro roared at Ninani. Then he shook out his mane and bounded down the stairs, taking five at a time. He landed on the moose's back and sunk his teeth into him.

The moose struggled, trying to shake off Cabaro. The lion bit down harder. Slowly, the moose sank to the ground. Cabaro released his grip and roared. The fur surrounding the lion's bite was drenched in blood.

"Tell him not to kill him!" Rollan said. "He's a friend."

"Some friend," Kirat murmured.

The lion moved off the moose's back, but only because Uraza had pushed him out of the way. The leopard had a few scratches from the moose's antlers but was otherwise unharmed.

Abeke looked at Olvan as he remained still on the stairs. "Is he . . . should we check–?"

"No point," Rollan said. "There's not much we can do for him, anyway." He held up his dagger. "Ready?"

Abeke nodded. "Which way are we heading?" she asked the guards.

"Straight ahead and to the left," the younger guard said.

Abeke counted to five, then ran down the stairs and took the last turn in the foyer.

It was a full-out brawl. There were only a few fortress guards remaining, with most of them lying on the floor . . . or worse, infected by Zerif's parasites.

"Don't let the parasites touch you," Abeke yelled as she let her first arrow fly. It landed in a Greencloak's leg. She quickly released another, this one finding its way to her side. Abeke didn't know this Greencloak, but that did not make the attack any less painful.

Abeke blocked a staff attack from another Greencloak. It was Errol! He had assisted in one of Abeke's first training exercises at Greenhaven. Uraza had already jumped on Errol's spirit animal. Uraza shook the lemur hard before flinging it against the wall. Errol momentarily paused, turning toward his animal. That gave Abeke a chance to jab an arrow into his chest, but not his heart.

"I'm sorry," she whispered as he fell to the ground.

Rollan sliced his Greencloak in the stomach as Essix picked up his lizard spirit animal. "Where's Kirat?" he yelled, spinning around.

"There!" Abeke said, pointing. She started toward Kirat, then stumbled as she saw who was ahead. "No!"

A few steps away, Kirat fought one-on-one with Finn, their friend from North Eura. Cabaro faced off against his black wildcat. Finn, usually a pacifist, had once been one of the Greencloaks' best warriors. And Kirat was actually holding his own against him! Kirat may have been even better than Meilin with a sword, although Abeke would never say that to either of them.

"Can you shoot him in the shoulder?" Rollan asked. "Like you did with Olvan?"

Abeke nocked an arrow, then shook her head. "They're moving too fast. I might hit Kirat my mistake."

"But it's Finn!" Rollan said. "Kirat will kill him!"

Donn, Finn's wildcat, sunk its teeth into Cabaro's leg. The lion whimpered, causing Kirat to falter. That gave Finn an opening, and he took it, slicing a gash into Kirat's arm. The boy screamed but didn't drop his sword.

Abeke raised her bow. She didn't want to hurt Finn. He was their friend. A fellow Greencloak. But she also had to protect Kirat.

Tasha and Ninani reached Finn before Abeke could release the arrow. As Finn swung at her, Tasha arched backward, ducking his sword. She swung her staff low, striking Finn in the knees. Then she hit him across the head, knocking him unconscious.

"I could have handled it," Kirat said as he inspected his arm.

"You're welcome," Tasha replied.

"Back-to-back!" Rollan yelled. "That's the only way we're going to get out of here."

"There's no way we can make it to my father's study," Kirat said. Blood dripped from his wound and down his arm. He was leaving a trail of it behind him.

"Then we go out the front door," Abeke said. "Now move!"

The group slowly inched their way to the main entrance. The three guards caught back up with them and took flanking positions around the kids. Even though the guards looked to be in worse shape than Kirat, they were still fighting to protect him.

A few steps away from the door, an older Greencloak with a white beard flung himself at the group. The Greencloak flailed at them, but the guards easily pushed him away. As the man slid across the floor, Abeke tried to remember his name. It wasn't until she saw the giant tortoise beside him that she realized it was Erlan, the librarian. Was no one safe from Zerif's parasites?

"Get it off me!" the youngest guard yelled as he dropped his sword and began wiping at his face. But it was too late. A parasite had already made its way underneath the skin and was curling into a spiral on the guard's forehead. Abeke looked back at Erlan and caught a glimpse of the empty vial in his hand.

"Cut it out!" one of the other guards yelled, raising his sword.

"No," Rollan said. "It's too late."

The infected guard's eyes went blank. He roared at the group, then lunged at Kirat. The bearded guard jumped in the way, blocking him.

"We'll hold him off!" the bearded guard said as he struggled with the infected one. "Get out of here!"

They ran toward the main doors. "We're almost there!" Rollan yelled, hurdling over a shattered wooden chair.

"And then what?" Kirat asked.

"We make a break for the sailboat," Abeke said. "If we can make it there, we have a shot of getting off this island."

They smashed through the doorway, pushing infected Greencloaks out of their way. As Abeke glanced behind her to see if the others had followed, she saw a streak of red out of the corner of her eye. Then two more flashed among the green cloaks and the guards' silver chain mail.

Could it be . . . ?

She searched through the crowd, and finally, she saw them.

The Redcloaks.

Farther away, a group of them fought alongside Faisel's guards. Some had weapons, and some fought with their bare hands. Although they were few in number, they seemed to be holding their own.

"Follow me," one of the Redcloaks said, appearing beside Abeke. "We have a boat ready." Unlike the others, whose white masks were all fashioned in the shapes of animals, his was featureless. Abeke wasn't sure, but she believed that he was the same one who had saved them before in Stetriol.

As they raced across the courtyard, Kirat slammed to a stop. "Father!" He pulled away from the group and took off across the battlefield.

"Come back!" Rollan yelled. He tried to grab Kirat's arm, but just missed.

Across the way, Faisel himself was engaged in one-on-one combat with a hooded man in black.

The man turned, and Abeke gasped. Zerif.

Cabaro growled and pawed the ground before eventually following Kirat.

"You all head to the boat," the Redcloak said. "I'll get the boy and the lion."

"No," Abeke replied. "Take Tasha and Ninani to the ship. Rollan and I will get Kirat."

Tasha shook her head. "But—"

"This is not up for discussion," Abeke said. "Go!"

The Redcloak hesitated as he stared at her. Though Abeke couldn't see his face, she sensed that he wanted to argue. Finally, he nodded. "We'll wait as long as we can," he said, his voice surprisingly soft. Then he took Tasha's arm and led her away.

Abeke and Rollan took off across the courtyard. Uraza ran along with them, while Essix flew up above. Kirat had almost reached his father when an infected guard rammed into the boy, knocking him to the ground.

"Kirat!" Faisel screamed. He abandoned his fight and ran toward his son. With the merchant lord's back now to him, Zerif pulled a knife from his waistband and hurled it at Faisel. Even with all the other noise in the courtyard, Abeke heard the unmistakable sound of metal settling into flesh as Faisel fell to his knees.

Essix reached Kirat before Rollan and Abeke, and began to claw at the guard's face. Then Rollan leaped forward and sunk his dagger into the man's chest. The guard finally fell.

Abeke helped Kirat to his feet. "Are you hurt?"

"I'm fine!" he said, pushing her away. "But my father . . . !"

Abeke grabbed his shirt before he could rush off. "You can't help him if you're dead," she said.

Faisel remained facedown on the ground. Abeke couldn't tell if he was breathing or not.

"We must go," she continued. "Now! Do *not* let your parents' sacrifice be in vain."

"Leaving so soon?"

Abeke spun around and saw that Zerif had somehow flanked them and was now blocking the way to the pier. He held an unstoppered glass vial in one hand and a throwing dagger in the other.

She put herself in front of Kirat and reached for an arrow, but her fingers slid through empty air. Her quiver was empty.

Abeke gripped her bow in her hands like a club and readied herself for Zerif's attack.

But instead of charging forward, Zerif only smiled. He tilted the vial, and a parasite scurried out onto his hand.

"I've never liked you," Zerif said. "I'm going to march you right off a cliff as soon as I have you under my control."

Then he hurled the parasite at Abeke.

Everything moved in slow motion. Abeke readied herself to try to deflect the worm, knowing full well how improbable that would be. But before she could even swing her bow, Uraza leaped into the air—into the space between Abeke and the parasite.

"No!" Abeke shrieked. She dropped her bow and sprinted forward.

Uraza twisted and turned, then dropped to the ground, trying to paw the gray worm off her fur. But it was no use. It was already burying itself into her skin.

Suddenly, the leopard stopped wriggling. Her body went completely still. Then she rose slowly to her feet.

Abeke's mind went silent, and her skin became cold. No, not cold. She was beyond feeling any type of sensation, as if her arms, her legs, her entire body had ceased to exist.

She crumpled to the ground. She could barely think. She knew she needed to do something—anything—but her mind kept reaching into the void, searching for a connection that was no longer there.

She saw Zerif in front of her. His lips were moving, but she couldn't hear him. Her ears, like the rest of her body, refused to operate.

"Interesting," Zerif said as Abeke was finally able to focus in on his voice. "This is even better than walking you off a cliff." He stroked his beard. "Uraza. Kill her."

Uraza hunched her back and growled. Still paralyzed, Abeke tried to reach out again with her mind, to find the bond between her and her spirit animal. But there was nothing, not even the faint remnants of a connection.

Their bond had been severed completely.

Uraza, please. Hear me! She searched the leopard's violet eyes. It was as if the animal had never seen her before.

And then Uraza jumped toward Abeke, claws out and teeth bared. Abeke braced herself for the impact.

Cabaro leaped over Abeke and collided with Uraza. The two cats tussled and snapped at each other as they rolled across the ground.

If not for the lion, Uraza would have ripped her apart.

"Don't hurt her!" Abeke said. The paralysis that seized her lifted somewhat, allowing her to finally control her numb body.

"So who's next?" Zerif said breezily. He had already produced another black vial. "Cabaro? Essix?"

"No one," the red-cloaked warrior said. He stood behind Abeke, with a crossbow aimed at Zerif.

"Do you think you can shoot me before I throw this?"

"Do you want to take a chance and find out?" the Redcloak replied.

Zerif smiled.

A second later, Uraza disappeared with a flash. Zerif lifted up his shirt, admiring his new tattoo.

All the air emptied out of Abeke's lungs at once.

"Move. Now!" Rollan said.

Abeke just stared at Zerif—at the image of Uraza stretched across his side. She felt someone pulling her to her feet—the Redcloak—and they somehow made their way through the fighting. She heard him yelling instructions to the other warriors in red—first on the battlefield, and then on a small skiff. But it was as if Abeke was hearing him underwater.

Her heart, her soul, was still on the battlefield, with Uraza.

16

REDCLOAKS

ROLLAN WAS SPEECHLESS. THEY HAD ESCAPED YET again, but their freedom had come at a terrible price. Once they made it out of the channel, the Redcloaks had taken them to their ship. There were at least twenty of them on board. Rollan caught some of their names—Howl, Worthy, and Stead, to name a few. They seemed respectful enough to give Rollan and the others their space, but now it was time for some answers.

Rollan walked over to Tasha and Kirat as they sat at the base of a flight of wooden stairs. Tasha hummed a tune to herself while rebraiding her hair. Kirat aimlessly worked a knife against a piece of wood that he must have found lying nearby. Tasha had called Ninani back into her dormant state, but Cabaro remained out on the deck. The lion scowled every time the boat hit a rough patch of sea, but he didn't move from his position. Rollan wasn't sure if he remained out to comfort Kirat, or if he was still too proud to go into his passive state.

"You should go below and have someone tend to your

arm," Rollan said. Kirat had tied it off in an attempt to stop the blood flow, but the makeshift bandage was already seeped through. "We didn't rescue you just so you could die from blood loss."

"I didn't ask you to save me at all," he said. His voice was barely louder than a whisper. "I should have remained with my parents. Perhaps with my help, we could have stopped them."

"More likely, you would have ended up dead," Rollan said. "Or a slave to one of those parasites. We helped to save your life, Kirat. You should be grateful."

Kirat rose from the ground and jammed his knife into the wooden railing. "None of this would have happened if you hadn't shown up!"

"You know, I'm sick and tired off all your belly-aching," Rollan said. He got into the boy's face and jabbed his chest. "You had a good life, Kirat. A great life. But that life is over. Your parents and those men gave their *lives* to protect you. The least you can do is honor their sacrifice." He shook his head. "Now get downstairs and clean that wound."

Rollan turned and began to march away.

"Wait," Kirat said. His voice, while defiant, didn't carry the same arrogance as usual. "Who was the man that you and my mother were talking about? Who's Tarik?"

A wave of emotions flooded Rollan. He hoped it wasn't apparent on his face. He couldn't afford to break down in front of Kirat. "He was a Greencloak. One of the finest men that I have ever known." He paused and took a deep breath to help settle his nerves. "He was also your uncle. Most of us hope to be half the Greencloak he was." Rollan could feel the pressure building behind his eyes. He was losing it. "He . . . he gave his life for me. He—"

"Rollan, it can wait until later," Tasha said. She rose from the ground and placed her hand on Kirat's shoulder. "Come on. I'll help you with your wound."

Rollan nodded at Tasha and watched them disappear below. He saw why Ninani had come to her. They both seemed to know just when someone needed a helping hand.

Rollan pulled the pendant that LaReimaja had given him from his pocket.

A bronze oval with two intersecting lines. LaReimaja had said it was the symbol of life. The pendant had been handed down from generation to generation in her family, and she wanted Rollan to give it to Kirat when he was "ready."

Rollan had pressed LaReimaja more about this, but the woman had just smiled and said that Rollan would know.

He pocketed the pendant and moved to the other side of the ship. Abeke stood along the rail, her gaze fixated on Zourtzi. The fortress was barely visible, but they could still see the smoke rising into the sky.

"How are you?" he asked.

She shrugged. "Empty. Lost. Alone."

Rollan wrapped his arm around her shoulder. Her skin was like ice. "You're not alone," he said.

Abeke gave him a blank stare. "She was there, and then in the space of a heartbeat, she was gone. She looked at me like I was a stranger. It was as if our bond had never existed."

"We'll get her back," Rollan said. "I promise."

Abeke and Rollan turned as someone approached them. It was the head Redcloak. The one with the faceless mask. The one who had saved them, time and time again.

"Is everyone in your party okay?" he asked. He may have been speaking to them both, but Rollan noticed that he was only looking at Abeke.

"We'll survive," Rollan said, answering for both of them. "Now, how about explaining what's going on here?" He crossed his arms. "We need some answers."

"Soon," the Redcloak said. "Be patient. We're taking you somewhere safe."

"Yeah, and where is that?" Rollan asked. "If you haven't noticed, nowhere seems to be safe anymore. Zerif can get to us anywhere. In Zourtzi, in Stetriol, and even at Greenhaven."

The Redcloak sighed. "So the rumors are true," he said. "Greenhaven has fallen as well." He looked out at the sea. "You should rest. There will be more battles to come."

"At least tell us your name," Abeke said. "You've saved our lives again and again." She took a step forward. "Tell us who you are, so we can thank you properly."

The Redcloak hesitated. "I'm called King," he said. "I am the leader of the Redcloaks."

Abeke offered him a slight bow. "Thank you. We are forever in your debt."

King began to walk away, but stopped.

He slowly turned around and stared at Abeke. "I used to be known by another name." He reached behind his head and slowly unfastened his mask. "You knew me as Shane."

Rollan stumbled a step backward. It *was* Shane, but he wasn't the same as when Rollan had last faced him. His eyes were yellow, like a crocodile's.

Abeke inched forward. "You!" she hissed. "I should have known! You're somehow behind all of this, aren't you?" She pulled back her sleeve, then gasped. Rollan realized that she had tried to call Uraza, but of course the leopard was no longer here. "It doesn't matter," she said, balling her hands into fists. "I'll face you with or without Uraza."

Rollan grabbed Abeke's arm before she could swing. "Calm down," he said. "He just saved our lives."

Abeke shook Rollan off. "And do you remember the last time Shane *saved my life*? He used it as a way to sneak into Greenhaven and betray us."

"That was before," Shane said. "A lifetime ago. Much has changed . . . obviously." His gaze had fallen to his feet, his yellow crocodile eyes small and sad. He let out a deep breath, then returned the mask to his face. "I know this is difficult, but I need you to trust me. To trust us," he said. "There's something you need to see. It may be the key to saving Erdas, and perhaps the key to saving Uraza as well." He took a step forward and looked out across the water. "We sail to the Place of Desolation."

Varian Johnson is the author of six novels for children and young adults, including the middle-grade capers *The Great Greene Heist* and *To Catch a Cheat*. A former structural engineer, he now lives outside of Austin, Texas, with his family and two cocker spaniels.